SA - 286

A. A. McClymont

iUniverse, Inc.
New York   Bloomington

SA - 286

iUniverse books may be ordered through booksellers or by contacting:

iUniverse
1663 Liberty Drive
Bloomington, IN 47403
www.iuniverse.com
1-800-Authors (1-800-288-4677)

ISBN: 978-1-4502-6843-1 (pbk)
ISBN: 978-1-4502-6844-8 (ebk)

Library of Congress Control Number: 2010916060

Printed in the United States of America

iUniverse rev. date: 11/3/2010

Dedication

To the Officers and men and women of the United States of America Armed Forces, who every day place their lives on the line to defend our privileges.

Acknowledgments

I thank my parents for encouraging me with my writing as a child and as an adolescent, and for creating the conditions that made me an avid reader of fiction and non-fiction; and I thank my youngest daughter Ashley for proofing and editing the manuscript, and for improving, and adding to, the text, making the story more interesting.

CHAPTER 1
BAD NEWS

THE BLACK FOUR-DOOR SEDAN stopped short of the telephone pole across the street, the two men got out and walked towards the house. Looked like a Ford, year old, maybe two, could use a wash. The tall man wore a dark suit and a dark tie and carried a manila envelope and a cellular phone in his right hand, the other man wore tan pants and a sports jacket, no tie, and turned his head twice to look at the parked car. The men stopped at the fence and the tall one made a phone call, spoke no more than ten seconds and put the phone in its belt holder. Harmless looking, business-like, but just the same John turned off the vacuum cleaner and walked to the gray stuffed chair next to the low bookcase and pulled his Browning semi-automatic from under the cushion, released the magazine, made sure that it was full, pressed it back with the palm of his left hand, forced the slide to place one round in the chamber, made sure the safety was on and hid the pistol in his short's right pocket. Not much wrong with the two guys, but better overcautious than dead.

The house phone rang. John checked the time, ten minutes before noon. Two men were standing on the sidewalk, facing each other. "This is John."

— "John, it's Steve Kowalski in Chicago." Funny, John had not heard from Steve Kowalski in seven years and Steve was not supposed to know his telephone number.

— "Steve? What's going? Don't tell me you're finally getting married and want me at the wedding." Steve was in his mid fifties and a bachelor, never married and a notorious ladies man. "You finally surrendered?"

1

— "There are two men in your driveway. Please talk to them." Curt, no small talk, almost unfriendly, very unlike-Steve. "Sorry, we'll talk later." Shit, it does not sound good, maybe they found Kopernik's teeth.

The two men remained next to the fence. John walked to the entrance door, opened it and motioned them to come in. The grass needed to be cut, the small palms John had planted four weeks earlier seemed healthy enough. The front lawn looked empty compared to those in the neighborhood, the back yard was John's pride, two mango trees that gave good fruit, papayas, four lemon and one grapefruit trees, four raised planting beds with tomatoes and melons and a hard-to-control patch of bamboo to the left of the pool. The tall man spoke.

— "I'm Craig Prentice of the Orlando Police Department, this is Doctor Menendez, we've been asked to come talk to you by friends of yours in Chicago. I'm afraid we have bad news, very bad news, May we come in?" Prentice did not wait for John to answer, he walked though the door and the doctor followed. "May we sit down?" John sat on the gray stuffed chair and motioned the other two to the sofa. They sat down.

— "What bad news?" John had moved from Chicago to Orlando seven years earlier, two months after retiring from the Chicago Police Department. His son Jack lived in Chicago and his daughter Patricia, married to an Army Major, was now stationed in Frankfurt, Germany. "Not one of the kids, for God's sake."

— "I'm afraid it is one of your children, your son." Doctor Menendez had a soft voice.

— "My son, what? Can't be." Menendez must be the in-house psychiatrist, they sent a psychiatrist, they expect me to break down. "I talked to my son three days ago, he's coming over next month. They're taking a vacation in the keys." For years John had not spoken with Jack, until Patricia flew with Jack to Orlando unannounced and both of them stayed for four days and talked little about what mattered; during the last two years John saw Jack twice in Chicago and once in Orlando, when Jack and his partner stopped for two days on their way to Fort Lauderdale to board a cruise ship, and lately John's relationship with Jack had warmed up, especially during the last two phone calls that lasted longer than any of the talks they ever had.

— "Your son is no longer with us. I'm afraid I can't put it any better than that. His partner is gone too." Doctor Menendez had sat at the edge of the sofa and now leaned forward with his hands together as if praying and clapped softly. Detective Prentice was leaning back with his face down, staring at his knees.

"It happened yesterday or the day before, they are not clear on that yet, they just found them. Captain Kazmierski called our boss and we drove to see you immediately, I'd say they were found no more than two hours ago, three at the most. We've been asked to drive you to the airport, one of Captain Kazmierski's men is airborne and will be landing at two-thirty and both of you are booked to leave for Chicago an hour later. You'll be in Chicago by seven this evening."

— "What happened?" It was as if a hand grenade had gone off in front of John's face, he could not think, his mind was closed. John's eyes went to Jack's photograph on top of the bookcase, his graduation picture at Notre Dame. What a great looking kid! Jack's hair was long then, long curly hair framing the blue eyes he got from his mother. Skinny Jack. Happy years then, Jack getting an intern job in the Loop before going to business school, Patricia a sophomore at the University of Illinois always in love with some guy that owned a guitar, Maureen's second book doing well. "What happened to Jack?"

It was Prentice that answered, his eyes fixed on his knees, acting as if he was embarrassed, maybe he was. For a big guy he had a tinny voice. "All we know is that your son and his partner were found dead in their house earlier today; they may have been dead for some time, they don't know yet. The detective that will fly with you will be updated as soon as he lands and he'll be able to brief you, I'm sorry I can't be of more help." The manila envelope was on Prentice's right side.

— "What's in the envelope?"

— "It's not for you, it's mine, I have to mail it, I don't know why I took with me. I should have left it in the car, I'm sorry, I'm very upset. I'm very sorry about your loss. We know you're a brother officer, if there is anything we can do we will." No doubt that Prentice was upset. "I'm going to help myself to a glass of water."

It happened with no warning, John started to cry, making small sounds, tears flowing and his nose running on both sides. John cried because Jack was dead and he cried because he had not told him that he loved him, that he loved him the way he was, that he had always loved him, that he had been a fool for not accepting him. First Maureen and now Jack. Why? Why Jack? Why not him? Jack was a young man with a whole life ahead, while he was marking time with his plants and his tennis and his golf and his television and old movies, spending half of his days with people he hardly knew and with whom he had not much in common. No illusions either, just memories.

— "Was it an accident?"

Doctor Menendez answered: "No."

— "Was it a suicide?"

— "We don't know. You'll have to wait for the detective joining you. We have no information." Prentice was back with two glasses of water and ice, he gave one to John and one to the doctor. "You may want to pack some clothes if you plan to stay in Chicago. What you have in your pocket you'll have to give to your companion, he has a badge and he'll get it through security". So much for John's concealed weapon.

They made the airport an hour before Flight 284 from Chicago arrived. John had sat in the rear seat by himself and had cried most of the time; he did not fully gain his composure but forced himself to keep a stiff upper lip once they parked. He thanked Prentice and Menendez and kept thinking that for a veteran detective he had behaved like a wimp. Well, I am who I am, take me or leave me. The airline gave John and Lieutenant Barkeley a courtesy upgrade to first class. Barkeley was not as tall as John and was overweight, John figured five-foot-ten at most, two-hundred-and-eighty pounds, a forty-six waist, unshaven, with a big head and a round red face and hardly a neck, a heart attack waiting to happen. When Barkeley spoke he looked at John's chin, what made John uneasy; he spoke very low and it was hard to make up what he said. Each had two little bottles of Jack Daniels and a plastic cup full of ice in front of them, no food.

— "Captain Kazmierski will be waiting for us at O'Hare. I spoke to him when I landed. You want me to tell you what he knows so far?" John nodded. "First let me tell you that the entire department is on this case, the Captain moved everything else to the back burner. The cleaning lady found the two boys this morning, she comes every Wednesday, has a key, called 911, a patrol car drove up, the officers found your son and his friend dead sitting on a sofa, four bullet wounds each, small bore, no exit, no signs of violence." Barkeley spoke as if he were reading a report about the disappearance of an used car, to say that he was detached of feeling would be an understatement, maybe that was why Kazmierski chose Barkeley to go to Orlando. "You all right with this?" Did not wait for an answer. "No weapon found. Two shots in the chest, two in the head, a professional job. I was not at the crime scene, I'm only relating what I've been told on the phone." It was as if Barkeley was saying 'don't blame me if I'm wrong, I'm just the messenger'. He continued in a very low voice and John had to lean over and noticed Barkeley's strong breath. "Nothing taken. All lights off. That's that, I know nothing more." Barkeley must have felt that he had fulfilled his duty and said no more, had his two drinks without pause and asked "You have any questions?" John shook his head. "You was in the department until when?"

— "Seven years ago. I retired with twenty-five. Signed in right after the Marine Corps." John had entered the Police Academy immediately after the service with the intention of going to Law School at night, but never did. By the time John left the Academy Maureen had changed from a kid in the neighborhood to a young woman of twenty-one. They dated and married a year later. They had Jack in eleven months and Patricia two years later, to the day. Two kids, same birthday, Jack always complained that Patricia got all the attention.

It was cold in Chicago. They arrived at United Terminal and met Captain Kazmierski waiting at the gate, in plain clothes. Eugene Kazmierski was a lieutenant when John retired, he and his wife Donna had been friends of John and Maureen for years. The Captain's eyes were very red, no doubt he had cried earlier; he had known Jack since this was a child.

— "John, I have no words. It is as if Jack were my boy. There is nothing I can say to you. Donna wants you to come stay with us. What is the world coming to? What in Heaven is wrong? How can this be?" He embraced John and caused the people coming out of the gate to slow down and walk around them. They did not speak much in the Terminal. John had to retrieve his one suitcase before boarding the unmarked car parked at the curb. Captain Kazmierski sat in the back seat, to John's left. "I called Germany and spoke to the officer in charge, it's eight hours later there, early evening when I called, the Base Commanding Officer called me back, a Colonel, he was going to talk to Tricia right then. By now she sure knows."

It was a very awkward moment, the two of them not knowing what else to say. "Sergeant Miller is driving us, he'll stay with you. Are you up to visit Jack's house? You may see something we didn't. They removed the kids earlier, after the photographs. You tell me. Are you going to be all right?" John nodded. Sergeant Miller drove fast into the City and to Jack's house, six blocks west of the Water Tower. The area in front of the house, all the way to the curb, had been cordoned off with yellow tape. A parking spot had been saved for them across the street. There were two patrol cars, one van and several officers on the sidewalk, two who John recognized and came forward to say a few words. The rest remained as they were as Captain Kazmierski passed by with his companion and entered the house.

— "Gene, pretend it isn't Jack, pretend we are working a case. It'll be easier on both of us."

CHAPTER 2
THE SCENE

JACK'S HOME IS A three-story townhouse, about thirty foot wide, with a recently sand-blasted light gray stucco façade that stands out from the rest of the houses on both sides of the street that have not been cleaned for years, if ever, and are several shades of gray darker. Two steps up to reach the first floor, a wide single wood door painted black, one large window on each side of the door, four narrower windows at second and third floor levels. A very geometric design.

The entrance door opens to the left into a long, narrow vestibule with a terrazzo floor of very shiny checkered white and black tiles laid on a diagonal. The only furniture two wood benches placed end to end on the left side with at least a dozen pair of shoes, all sort of shoes, under them. A row of hooks on the wall across from the benches, a little higher than eye level with one tan raincoat and a dark blue ski jacket hanging next to each other. No hooks for children. At the end of the vestibule a single door with four glass panels separated by narrow wood strips leads to one large space with a very dark, almost black, wood plank floor also laid diagonally. The rear wall of the large space is covered by a beige cloth drape that extends floor to ceiling the full length of the wall. On the right side of the vestibule a large kitchen with cabinets and appliances on both sides, all vertical surfaces stainless steel and the horizontal surfaces a mix of stainless steel and black laminate, lit from the ceiling and by lights hidden under the wall cabinets. Conspicuous on one of the walls a black and white poster of Jack and Christian smiling and wearing chef's aprons and hats.

To the left of the vestibule a not-too-large room furnished as an office with one modern-looking metal desk with a glass top in the center of the room and a comfortable-looking chair behind it, three file cabinets against one of the walls and two chairs in front of the desk. On the desk a telephone, a Dell laptop computer with its lid down, a calendar, a digital clock that matches the calendar, a very pretty lamp with a wide, low, black shade and a stainless steel open box about eight-inch square and an inch high with a stapler, a tape dispenser and a container with pens and pencils in it, all pointing up, everything arranged in the most orderly geometric pattern. A very sterile-looking desk with neither writing paper nor a notebook. Three drawers on each side of the desk, no locks. To the right of the desk a black waste basket, empty. To the left, a heavy-looking shredder, also empty. Not a speck of dust, not a mark on the glass top, as if it had never been used.

On the wall opposite the large window that opens to the street two groups of photographs, all the same size, all framed in the identical thin black metal frames with white mats, the group to the left with Maureen, Maureen and John, Maureen and Tricia, Tricia and her two children and Tricia and Jack. The other group with one older woman and men that John could not identify, except for Christian in three of the frames. Behind the desk, a black-and-white poster, unframed, of Jack and Christian in tennis clothes, probably two or three year old. Both were smiling and looked hansom. Later on, a printer and a machine that serves as a copier and fax were discovered inside one of the cabinets. Hanging from one of the chairs an empty leather briefcase.

John and Captain Kazmierski had been joined by Sergeant Carol Mackenzie, a nine-year veteran, who was in charge of the crime scene. John did not remember Carol but thought that her name sounded familiar. The two men had taken their coats off and the three of them were wearing plastic gloves and plastic covers on their shoes and heads. Fingerprints had been lifted earlier and every space had been photographed and video-taped, but just the same they followed protocol.

They started on the rear part of the third floor, in the main bedroom with two identical dressing closets. The bathroom had a whirlpool and a sauna; white marble floor, all surfaces black and white, white and tan towels. Most surfaces were covered with the white powder used to enhance and lift fingerprints, the mirrors and the shower door completely covered with white powder. Two very low full-size beds in the bedroom, three night tables, one between the beds and one on each side, all cherry wood of modern design, white walls, wood parquet floor. Nothing on the night tables but a white telephone. A small bookcase, two shelves of books, framed photographs and an alarm clock. Two colorful Botero prints of grotesque people on one of the walls and behind the bed a square black-and-white poster of Jack and Christian in profile, with a black background, facing each other, taken from mid-chest up; an eerie sight. Both closets were inhumanly neat, sweaters folded to the same width and piled by color and shade; pants, shirts and jackets in separate compartments in equally-spaced hangers, hats in one of the closets, nothing out of place, each closet resembling a boutique, except for one pair of tan corduroy pants hanging from a hook on the wall in the closet to the left. Many shoes in both closets, dress shoes, athletic shoes, boat shoes. John checked the pockets in the corduroy pants and all he found was seventy-two dollars in folded bills. No wallets, no cellular phones, not a scrap of paper.

— "Did you find their wallets, telephones?" John asked.

— "No. There isn't anything in any pocket. We checked drawers, all the jackets, all the pants. Nothing hidden in between clothes, nothing of interest in the night tables. There are watches in both closets, look in the small drawers, rings, bracelets." Sergeant Mackenzie answered.

On the front of the third floor, facing the street, a smaller bedroom with sparse modern furniture and a closet with wood doors that extends the entire length of one wall, empty except for pillows, two Chagall prints, a low bookcase with a few paperbacks. A small bathroom. Not so much white dust here. The second room looked unused.

The stairs were narrow, made of dark wood, no carpeting, attached to the left side wall. The handrail and the steps had been dusted. Framed black and white photographs on the wall on the side of the stair, people, birds, sailboats. The second floor extended only over one-third of the house footprint, facing the street, as the remainder had been left open to create a double-height space for the living room in the first floor. It was obvious that the house had been gutted and remodeled. John had not seen Jack's house before and new of it only from references from Jack and Tricia. It was more attractive than he expected, but with a sterile feeling. Jack and Christian had bought the house four years earlier and had spent a year and a half remodeling it, and obviously quite a lot of money. What a shame! On the second floor there are two rooms of equal size and a small bathroom, one room empty, the other contained four upholstered chairs distributed over a Persian rug facing a large flat television screen hung on one of the side walls, a small refrigerator, a low table with magazines on it and a bookcase on the wall opposite the television screen, the shelves filled with CDs and DVDs, music and movies. John bent to read the tittles, many were familiar. On top of the bookcase another Dell laptop, with the top up but not turned on. Everything had been dusted, including the computer screen.

John observed but did not touch anything. They were now on the first floor, where the two dead men had been found. Under the stair John saw the control of a security system. In an open cubicle an upright computer and a router with an antenna on top and a fax machine, ostensibly the receiver for e-mails, feeding the laptops around the house through the antenna.

— "They found them here, right?"

— "On the sofa closest to the pool table." Sergeant Mackenzie answered.

— "What do you make of the security system?"

— "Sophisticated. The cleaning lady knew the pass-code, November4, they changed the code every month and used the name of the month followed by a number at the end. We had a technician come over from the security company to explain the system to us and had him change the code to Chicago."

The tree of them were standing with their backs to the door to the vestibule, the kitchen to their right. The back wall was fully covered by a drape, all lights were on. In front of the drape, to the left a pool table, to the right two large gray sofas, facing each other, and a coffee table with a glass top in between, white powder everywhere. The sofas had been covered with sheets of thin transparent plastic. There were no blood stains. Two squarish leather and chrome chairs, many lamps. Between the sofas and the kitchen a dining table also with a glass top and eight upright chairs upholstered in a shade of gray darker than the sofas. Nothing on the table except white powder. The kitchen all stainless steel and black, the refrigerator very wide, two dishwashers which seemed odd to John who washed his plates by hand, a commercial-looking stove with eight burners and two ovens underneath, two wine coolers with glass doors, white powder everywhere.

— "All right if I look into the garbage?"

— "It'll be best if I do it, better don't touch, I don't want some defense lawyer complaining that the scene has been contaminated by a civilian." Sergeant Mackenzie answered. "There is s a trash compactor to the right of the sink. We took the bag with the rest of the evidence, very little in it, practically empty."

— "What day they collect the trash?"

— "I'll find out today." Shit, first oversight. Lieutenant O'Rourke was living up to his reputation.

— "Recycling bags?"

Sergeant Mackenzie felt the pain of her inattention. "Did not look for them, sorry."

— "Don't worry about it." John had sensed Carol's discomfort. "Let's check the cabinets, you do it."

The third tall cabinet door Sergeant Mackenzie opened revealed three gray plastic garbage bins, one nearly full of plastic items, one half-full with newspapers, the third nearly filled with glass bottles. "I will have the van back in half an hour, we'll take the three to the lab."

— "Sergeant, don't mind me but I did your job for more years that I'm willing to admit. You want to make sure the bottles don't shift in the bin, we are most interested in those on top. It'll be best if you get a crew here and pull the bottles one by one and number them, photograph each level and make a sketch showing their position in the bin, level by level. There is drawing and a form for showing position in one of the procedural manuals."

— "I know. It's an old manual, I had to read it for a test."

— "Sergeant, I resent 'old'. I'm the one who wrote it." John gave Sergeant Mackenzie a fake smile. "Is there a basement?"

— "Come we'll show you." Carol walked towards a door under the staircase that John had expected to hide a closet. The door opened to a wood stair leading to an exercise room with two stationary bicycles and two other exercise machines, a tall metal cabinet with four lockers and a stainless steel refrigerator covered with white powder; inside water bottles, health drinks and a white ceramic bowl with six oranges. The walls were paneled with yellow pine placed vertically and the floor carpeted with gray tweed. Aligned on one of the walls two clothes washers and two clothes driers, nothing in them, one long shelf with soap bottles and two plastic bins with soiled towels. Three doors, one door leads to a sauna, larger than the one upstairs, another to a bathroom with two showers. The third door opens to a mechanical room located between the exercise room and the street, with air conditioning equipment, a water heater, an electric generator and two 150-gallon oil tanks side by side; John checked the gages, both tanks were full. All together the basement was no more than half of the first floor footprint.

The last thing they did before leaving was to draw the drapes in the living room to expose a glass wall leading to a garden that extends the width of the house and maybe twenty feet to the back, paved with squares of dark gray slate, with many large pots with plants that were covered with heavy plastic. John could see two fig trees under the plastic. In the rear a stainless-steel barbeque, a teak table and several chairs that had faded to a very light gray. They closed the drapes and turned all lights off as they left.

It was one in the morning. They ate at a pizzeria two blocks away and John rode with Captain Kazmierski to spend the night at his house.

— "I spoke to my brother Patrick earlier, he'll make the funeral arrangements. Patrick already sent an obituary for tomorrow's papers, he drafted it and a friend of his faxed it to the papers. I said we'll have a service at the funeral house and I insisted on a reception in a restaurant. Patrick wanted it to be at his house, but I insisted on a restaurant; Patrick will take care of it in the morning. I said I'll be spending the day with you and I'll see them tomorrow night; they want me to stay at their house."

— "Whatever works for you, John." Captain Kazmierski paused, uneasy. "You know I need you to identify the body, you know that. Very early tomorrow, they'll wait for us, you know there has to be an autopsy".

— "I'm OK with it. First thing, we'll get up at six." John did not expect to be able to sleep and he was right.

— "Why a restaurant? Why not Patrick's house?

— "I only want to make sure that it's a place easy to get in and easy to mix with other people, a relaxed atmosphere, where anybody can move around. I want to be sure that whomever killed my son comes to the funeral and feels at ease. From what you've told me so far it doesn't look to me that Jack and Christian were killed by a stranger, it has to be somebody they knew, somebody they let into their house. A friend, an acquaintance. He who killed Jack and Christian has to be at the wake or he'll be noticed for his absence." There was anger in John's voice. "And you will arrange for your two cleverest guys to photograph everybody.

CHAPTER 3
MONTY

THE PAIN JOHN FELT identifying Jack's body is the pain he will measure all pains against for the rest of his life. John saw the two small entry bores on Jack's forehead, one above Jack's right eye, the other in between the eyes, and could not force himself to look at the chest wounds. Jack's face was pale and serene, his eyelids closed, his thin lips grayish white. John signed the form and walked out. It was ten minutes past eight when they left. The autopsies had been scheduled to start at 0800 HS.

As John and Captain Kazmierski entered the briefing room, those who knew John from his years on the force had few words to say, the new ones shook John's hand and three old friends hugged him. There were diagrams drawn on three rectangular white boards pinned on the rear wall, one a schematic plan of Jack's living room showing the sofas, the pool table and other furniture outlined in black, the position of the bodies outlined in blue and numbered one and two, red lines showing the trajectories of the eight projectiles based on an analysis of the bodies positions and on the points of entry, and the best estimate of the assassin's positions marked with red crosses. There were three red crosses, one behind the sofa closest to the garden, half way between the bodies, the other two between the sofa and the coffee table. The other two posters showed the bodies outlined in black, the trajectories in blue and the different angles of the eight shots referred to the vertical and to a horizontal line drawn perpendicular to the sofa. The two last diagrams had been used to construct the first board.

— "For those of you who do not know me, I'm Doctor Robert Chan, I'm a forensic psychologist. The diagrams on the wall are the product of the work of my people and is ongoing. You don't need to take notes, we'll be distributing a brief shortly and you'll receive daily updates as more is learned and analyzed." Dr. Chan had his back to the diagrams, had placed both hands on the table in front of him and was leaning forward. "Let's make this clear. We all know one of the victims is John O'Rourke's son and John is one of us, a twenty-five year veteran, John is family, this is personal, enough said." Dr. Chan looked straight to one of the men in the rear of the room and moved his eyes to others until he reached the front row. There were some twenty men in the room and three women, all detectives. "Ask questions when I'm finished. Write them down and wait. Understood?" Dr. Chan did not wait for an answer. "We will have more information at the end of today, once the autopsies reports are reviewed, we think about six this evening, we're taking no breaks." He paused. "Lieutenant O'Rourke's son is Number One." He paused again. "The first two shots were fired from behind the sofa. The assassin was standing half way between the victims, closest to Number Two, no more than one foot behind the sofa, if that much. The assassin is right handed. He shot Number Two one inch above his left ear, then turned his weapon towards Number One who was turning his head to his right as he heard the shot, and shot Number One above his right eye. With the two victims wounded, possibly dead or at least shocked, the assassin moved around to face the sofa, stood in front of Number Two and shot him once in the forehead and twice in the chest, in the heart. All three shots with the barrel touching Number Two's skin or clothes. Based on the size of the entry boreholes, the preliminary assessment is that the assassin used a 22-caliber weapon, I stress preliminary, we'll have conclusive information later on." Dr. Chan looked at John before continuing, John looked at the floor. "The assassin moved in front of Number One and did the same, one shot in the forehead and two in the chest. You would assume from the number and location of the shots that the assassin is a professional. No casings were found, and that reinforces the notion." Dr. Chan moved to be in front of the table and leaned backwards on it with his hands on either side of his body. "It is my group's opinion that the assassin is an acquaintance of the deceased. For there is no sign of physical violence, barely a reaction form Number One as he heard the first shot, we assess he turned to his right surprised. The coffee table, the dining table and the desk top in the first floor's office had been thoroughly wiped clean." Dr. Chan was perspiring and used a handkerchief on his forehead. "There were neither glasses nor bottles on the coffee table, or in the kitchen, as you would expect when a friend visits. We believe nothing was taken from the house, there are expensive watches and cash in the bedrooms, three laptops in plain view, and robbery is not the case." The few questions that followed were for clarification only and John, who had gone one step pass Doctor Chang's summary and had a further conclusion that he thought relevant, did not want to outshine the detectives and kept his thought to himself. And later on, other than to Captain Kazmierski, John made no mention of it. Nobody left the room, they watched the crime scene video and finally they turned to review the photographs, more than two hundred of them. Sandwiches, pizza and sodas arrived at five o'clock and at six Doctor Chan was back.

— "Listen up. The preliminary autopsies reports are still being looked over by my group but what I'll be telling you now is more or less final. There are tests results that will not be ready for three or four days. The weapon is a 22-caliber semi-automatic." Doctor Chan paused to glance at John. "There is no exit wound for any of the projectiles and there is a lot of tissue damage with each shot. Both reports indicate that the first shot caused death in both victims. There is more. All the shots were fired with the barrel in a horizontal or near horizontal position, which reveals that the assassin is either very short, child size, or that he bent or kneeled for the chest shots. At any rate we can not estimate the assassin's height from the trajectories." Doctor Chan glanced at John again. "The spectrometer results of the skin burns indicate that the munition is American or Canadian made, common stock, the stuff you purchase at any gun shop. Sergeant Mackenzie has more to say."

— "You all know me, but for the record, I'm Sergeant Carol Mackenzie, I'm in charge of the crime scene." Sergeant Mackenzie stood in front of the table with a manila folder in her left hand. She pulled out eight black and white photographs and went around the table to pin all of them on top of the diagrams. "The bodies were discovered by the cleaning woman at approximately 0900 HS Wednesday morning; she called 911, the call was logged at 0906 HS, all this is in the brief. The autopsies reports indicate time of death between 2020 HS and 2220 HS Monday night, with high reliability. Both of the deceased are public accountants, one worked for a private firm, the other for Cook County. Nobody in their places of work took notice that they did not show up on Tuesday. Early today we established from security tapes that Number One had left his place of work at 1812 HS; we were told he usually takes public transportation so we allowed between twenty and forty minutes and sat the time of arrival at home, assuming he went straight home, between 1840 and 1850 HS. From witnesses we know that Number Two left the American Gym at approximately 1830 HS and since the gym is three blocks away we sat the time of arrival at home at between 1845 and 1855 HS, provided he made no stops." Sergeant Mackenzie pointed to a photograph. "There is nothing in the refrigerator that suggests any of them brought home prepared food. The bag in the trash compactor is nearly empty,

15

there are no wrappings or bottles. But the autopsies reports indicate that both of the victims had eaten a variety of raw fish, that for now we'll characterize as sushi, rice, white bread, tomato, cucumber, hard cheese and anchovies, some undigested, others at an early stage of digestion. Forthcoming tests results may reveal more. Also, the autopsies reports indicate the presence of white wine in both victims." Sergeant Mackenzie could not say 'in both victims's stomachs' as it sounded macabre and Sergeant Mackenzie was sensitive to John been there. "Now, listen up, these four photographs show the upper layers of glass bottles in the recycling bin, none of them is white wine, they are all tea and fruit juices, only one bottle of red wine in the third level from the top. Where is the white wine bottle?"

Sergeant Mackenzie had made her first point, now to the second. "The last two photographs. Observe the shoes, they are light shoes, so-called boat shoes, both of the victims, and no socks. We checked the soles in both pairs, very clean. These shoes were not worn outside, only inside the house. Observe the clothes, light weight pants and Polo shirts, not the clothes you wear outdoors in Chicago in late November." Sergeant Mackenzie walked around the table and stood up in front of it. "Our preliminary conclusion is that the victims ate out and returned home with the assassin, changed shoes and clothes and sat down at the sofas. This suggests a high level of familiarity with the assassin. If they had eaten at home, we would have an empty bottle of white wine and the sushi containers in the trash compactor. I recommend we visit eating places in the neighborhood, emphasis on Asian places, in extending circles, and show photographs, someone may recognize the victims and lead us to the assassin." Sergeant Mackenzie gave the detectives a few moments to digest the information. "Comments?" Sergeant Mackenzie took a step back to lean on the table. "Lieutenant O'Rourke asked what day the trash is collected, it is Friday."

— "Are there security tapes at their work places?" It was Detective Madigan that asked.

— "Yes, both places. In a day or two we'll get copies."

— "Fingerprints on the water bottles. If they drank water it would not show in the reports." A new guy.

— "Being done."

— "Drugs?" Another young new guy.

Sergeant Mackenzie looked at John. "Specifically no hard drugs, but plenty of marihuana traces in both victims lungs. The reports indicate that both victims were habitual users."

— "Users?"

— "Both victims smoked marihuana frequently, and had done it for some time."

Captain Kazmierski read assignments from a list, several of the old timers huddled around John and made small talk and within twenty minutes everybody was gone. The traffic was heavy, being a Thursday night in Chicago. It was cold outside and John realized he would need to buy clothes heavier than his Florida outfits and a suit for the funeral too.

— "You know how it plays, John. It'll be a while before we pick up leads. If this is a professional job we may get a wind months from now from some disgruntled character, or some informer may pass a word to one of our guys and that may bring us to the assassin. For starts we have to search for motives, motive may be our best path. I suppose you haven't seen Jack much, Have any ideas?"

— "None so far. I've met Christian twice, I know Jack has, had, a good job, same firm since he finished school. I didn't know Christian worked for Cook County. I know they traveled plenty. They were coming to Orlando on their way to Key West next month, and I know they've been to Europe, France I think, at least twice in the last year and a half. On one trip the two of them visited Tricia in Germany, Jack promised to send me photographs. They've been on cruises too. You know, two young men with good jobs, no children, they had money to spend."

— "We'll be looking into their bank accounts, credit cards statements, telephone records, all of this has been requested, we'll have everything in one to three weeks, and we'll assign a team to paste their lives together. We'll go back six months first and then twelve months if we have to. You may have to sign authorizations. We'll find out if they made wills, there may be a motive there."

They were close to Captain Kazmierski's house. "Tomorrow I'll move to Patrick's house and I'll go clothes shopping. By the way, I did not want to come out like a rookie looking for the limelight so I kept this to myself, but I believe there were two people involved, could be three, but not just one. When the shooter was behind the sofa, why would Jack and Christian face the other way, the normal posture would be half turned, facing the person behind the sofa. The only reason for Jack and Christian to be looking forward is that they were conversing with those in front of them. What do you think?"

— "I think that you haven't lost your touch. I'll pass that along to Doctor Chang, he'll put in the next update. But I'll take the credit, I want to look as smart as you. You're good, John. You were good and you're still good. If you had not retired you'd be the captain."

— "Right, and if my Uncle Billy had tits, he'd be my Aunt Susan. 'If' is a very long word, Gene."

— "I'm going to detail Sergeant Miller to drive you, unless you prefer otherwise. Better yet, he'll drive you until you tell us different. He's a good kid, it'll do him good if you let some of your wisdom rub on him."

John arrived at his brother's house in mid- morning. In the afternoon Sergeant Miller drove John to the Mall where he bought a dark blue suit, shirts and much more he needed and was back at Patrick's house on time for dinner. John telephoned Patricia In Frankfurt, who would not be coming over, and arranged to visit with her the following week, and bought his ticket on the Internet for the coming Tuesday. There was a cremation ceremony on Saturday at Maschione Funeral House attended by family only and on Sunday morning family and friends gathered at the Green Dandy Pub for brunch. John met Jack's friends, drank with them and had miles of small talk, and kept a keen ear for any comment that may be revealing; there was none. Christian's family did not come to the brunch, as Christian's funeral was taking place simultaneously in Milwaukee, but Christian's father had called on Saturday and had arranged with John to meet for dinner in Chicago in two weeks. Jack's boss introduced himself to John and invited him to his office to retrieve Jack's personal belongings and John agreed to see him on Monday afternoon.

On Monday, Sergeant Miller drove John around for errands in the morning and after lunch he dropped John at Jack's place of work, the accounting firm of McAllister & Moyer Certified Public Accountants, where John was to meet Jack's boss, Monty DeSimone, General Manager, on the sixth floor, one of the three floors occupied by the firm. The reception area was luxurious, reflecting the importance and success of the firm, walls covered with light gray limestone, cherry trim, elegant chairs, many of them, glass coffee tables with business magazines. Two middle-aged receptionists dressed in tailored suits, one telephone operator attending to very busy phones. Big operation. If the reception area was meant to impress visitors, it did. John asked for Mr.

DeSimone and was told to please wait that Mr. DeSimone would come for him. A young woman also in a tailored suit brought a tray with a bottle of iced tea, a bottle of water and a crystal glass, all ice cold.

Monty was thin and on the short side, smartly dressed in a dark suit, white shirt and gleaming yellow silk tie. Tidy-looking, black shoes shined five minutes ago, not a wrinkle, short hair, graying on the temples, manicured hands, gold cuff-links. Monty's office was large with a wall-to-wall window with a view to the Sears Tower, an antique desk without a sheet of paper on it, a telephone with rows and rows of buttons and a table lamp identical to one John saw in Jack's house. One big chair behind the desk and in front two wing chairs upholstered in bright green; on the wall opposite the window a low credenza with an espresso machine that can make two cups at a time, no mugs. Not far from the machine a framed photograph of Monty shaking hands with President Reagan, both smiling. On the wall behind the desk one very large photograph of a magnificent sail boat with all sails full. Monty was a big wheel.

— "I can't tell you how much everybody here likes Jack. Myself and many others know Jack since he was an intern during his school years, he was as fine a young man as they come. A lot of fun and a fine accountant. Come, I'll walk you to Jack's office." Monty walked fast, in short steps.

— "Tell you the truth, I know very little of what Jack did, accounting I guess, taxes and the whole bit. Only during the last year we spoke more or less frequently, or at least more frequently than before, and Jack said something about what he was doing but I don't think I understood much."

— "Jack did not do taxes, his strength was doing enterprise analysis, balance sheet analysis, in plain words a company hires us to see what they are doing right and what doesn't work, what makes them money, what they should emphasize and what to abandon, and we, actually me, matches the company with a team of accountants that analyzes the operation. It's more business analysis, we call it consulting, than accounting per se, and a lot more interesting. Jack was very, very good at it, especially for his age. What was he?, Thirty, thirty-two? Jack's work reflected the experience of somebody much older. Your son was very accomplished."

— "Thirty-one."

— "A good looking young man too. Jack put his heart in his work, he put in long hours too."

— "What was Jack doing lately?"

— "For the last two and a half months Jack worked on a single project, a job that required much dedication as he had to do it alone. The company he analyzed is planning to go public, does not want it to be known for now, and insisted that a single person handled the job to keep it as confidential as one possibly can. A family owned firm, fine people, old fashioned, very lucrative business but the owner is on the other side of seventy and wants to ease out in a year or two. I know this people socially, that's how they came to us. And, of course because of our reputation; we've been in business in Chicago for eighty-two years, fifteen in this office, now we are in nine cities across the upper mid-west." Monty had to give his sales pitch.

— "Did Jack like his job? Was he happy?"

— "I have to say yes to both questions. Jack put his heart in his work, ask Mrs. Peterson, she was Jack's secretary, together with two other project managers."

— "Was that Jack's title?"

— "Yes. The second door to the left is Jack's office and the lady in the white vest is Mrs. Peterson."

The two walked into Jack's office, half the size of Monty's, without the luxury. One wood desk, one chair behind the desk, several file cabinets, a small window facing the street, one credenza matching the desk and a tall bookcase with every shelf full. John read a few of the titles, technical books, management, statistics. No photographs on the walls, two framed Modigliani prints with thin women with very pretty long faces. Cardboard boxes full of files on top of the desk and the credenza. A keyboard and an oversize monitor on the desk, only one wire coming out of the monitor disappeared through a hole near the rear edge of the desk. A wireless mouse sitting on a bright red mouse pad. John guessed the computer was on the floor under the desk. On a low table behind the desk a laser printer and a scanner.

— "Are you cleaning Jack's office?" It seemed too soon for John's taste.

— "Heavens, no. We're still not used to the idea that Jack is not with us". Monty meant dead, most people can not say the word. "I don't expect we'll use Jack's office for some time. Jack left it as you see it, we haven't touched a thing. Don't take it as a criticism but Jack was neater at home than at work. He was very intense all the time. May I offer you a cup of coffee, an espresso?"

— "That'll be nice, but let me look around, I've never seen my son at work. I think of Jack playing tennis or laughing, not working." John walked around the room. "I'll look into his drawers." Nothing of interest, folders, pens, three brand-new baseballs, a TV remote control, several bars of chocolate and, in the three drawers on the left, folded dress shirts, three ties, underwear and socks.

— "So, what happens to Jack's project? How will you finish it?"

— "Well, it's finished. I mean, it's not finished but it's finished. On his last day here Jack spent the afternoon with the company owner and the comptroller and gave them a progress report. Mr. Taylor stayed to have coffee with me as Jack was leaving, Jack's overall conclusion was that the company is run efficiently, Jack made recommendations to trim costs, and I added my advice that the next step is to talk to our tax guys in the seventh floor or they may see their added profits float east to Washington. An accountant's joke. I telephoned Jack at home and let him know Mr. Taylor was very happy with the results. " Monty pointed to one of the Modigliani's. "Would you like to carry them with you? Jack brought them here. I'm afraid that everything else is work stuff."

— "Yes, I'd like to. I don't have much that belongs to Jack. Maybe you'll have one of your people in the mail room wrap them for me, I'll pick them up next week, tomorrow I'm leaving for Germany to visit my daughter and two grandchildren. Only for one week."

— "Jack liked Germany. He visited last year."

John changed the subject. "Then Jack wrote a report. I'd be curious to read it, I'd like to see my son's work. If it's all right with you I mean."

— "That I can't do, I would lose my job. Jack gave the owners a progress report and they were happy with it, at least Mr. Taylor told me he was. I know from the questions Mr. Taylor asked me that his company will go public, and should do well. Anyways, Mr. Taylor liked Jack and was very upset when he heard the news of Jack's passing."

— "How did he find out?"

— "I telephoned the moment I was told by the police, I mean by your partners, I know you're a detective. A pair came here to ask at what time Jack had left the office. They asked for the security tapes too."

— "I'm retired; if you have to, you may characterize me as a poor golfer. I don't even talk about my tennis."

— "Mister Taylor was very upset about Jack's passing. I've known him for years, from the Yacht Club, we're both sailors. Well, I'm a sailor, Mister Taylor is a boater, big difference. I'm friends with Mister Taylor's daughter too, name is Julie. Smart woman, owns a catering company, operates our cafeteria and another one in the building, comes here often. I wish it were lunch time, you'd love it." Monty walked towards the door. "I'll go to my office and make us two cappuccini, you talk to Mrs. Peterson, she'll be happy to meet you, she knows Jack since he was an intern, she's been with us for at least two decades."

— "But I was very young when I started, never mind my four grandchildren." Mrs, Peterson was older than John, but dressed as a woman half her age. The only way to describe her desktop would be 'chaotic', not a square inch of desk top visible.

— "You look very busy."

— "Actually I'm not. I make a point of looking busy so they don't get rid of me. I've been here for so long that I make more than the junior accountants, it's becoming dangerous." Mrs. Peterson stood up from her chair and stretched up to hug John. "I loved your son very much, Jack was very nice to me, always brought me chocolates. We all loved him. We'll miss him much. Jack knew I enjoy gardening and printed articles from the Internet for me. I have three daughters and none of their husbands is half as nice as Jack. Your son was the best. We both like to read detective stories. Here, Jack gave me this one to read the last day I saw him, I finished it, now it's your turn." All of that Mrs. Peterson said in one breadth, John was sure she had rehearsed it.

— "And you're very sweet too Mrs. Peterson. I'm sure Jack liked you too." John took the book, 'The Client' by John Grisham, he'd seen the movie.

— "Call me Katie, and come see me any time."

— "I will, you may count on that." John followed the cappuccini's aroma to Monty's office. A porcelain cup and saucer were waiting on the edge of Monty's desk in front of one of the wing chairs.

— "The one behind you, that's not your boat, Is it?"

— "What your question means is that I can't afford it. Sorry, a sailor's joke. Actually, the boat is mine, at least eighty percent mine and I can not afford it. Before you ask, the bank owns the balance."

— "I did not mean…" John was embarrassed.

— "Of course you did not. It's an expensive-looking boat, and it is expensive, not a race boat really, but it has won many Lake Michigan races. In a modest way I'm a good sailor, I crewed for the America Cup years ago, younger days and all that. But the boat is my partner, unlike Jack I don't have a partner. Excuse my digressing, but it's better if you learn my facts from me rather than though gossip."

— "I …"

— "Mr. O'Rourke, Jack and I were long-time friends, not just co-workers, I went to Jack's house often for dinner or to shoot pool. Jack confided to me how you had changed your feelings toward him and how happy he was of getting together with you recently. I know all about it. My parents never accepted me. I was born and raised in Connecticut, came to Chicago to go to school and never left. My parents are dead now. I have to tell you that Jack was looking forward to going to Florida to see you." Drink your coffee, it'll get cold. Monty's eyes were misty. "Come see us when you come back from Germany, we'll have the paintings packed for you. I'm sorry, I can't talk any more."

John carried the book, the chocolate bars and the three baseballs in a plastic bag and had to wait for the elevator longer than he expected. When he got to the lobby John saw Mrs. Peterson turn around from facing the elevators and walk towards the street. She walked slow for John to catch up.

— "Don't look at me, let's walk to the corner, I have to tell you something." They stopped on the other side of the news stand. "You know Jack's job was very hush-hush." John nodded but did not answer and his silence compelled Mrs. Peterson to continue. "Jack did not tell me much but he told me that somebody was robbing these people blind. He said exactly that, somebody is robbing these people blind, word by word. Now, you're the detective, go find out what it means but keep it to yourself, I never said anything, I need my job." Mrs. Peterson put her arms around John's shoulders and pulled herself up to kiss him on the cheek. "Go find the one that killed our Jack and pull his eyes out."

CHAPTER 4
BOBBY

ON TUESDAY UNITED AIRLINES's Flight 944 to Frankfurt left on time at 1424 HS and arrived at Frankfurt International Airport at 0545 HS next morning. John worked on his notes for the first four hours of the flight, had a wonderful dinner, drank an extra half-bottle of Sauterne and had an extra dessert thanks to the young woman next to him who wishes to be thin. He watched the movie and slept the rest of the time, had breakfast before landing and met Patricia outside of customs. Patricia looked wonderful, had gained some weight, and Tony Junior and little Maureen were better looking than in any of their photographs. Tricia and Tony lived off base in a suburb that looked like Des Plaines. Two-story house, two-car garage, backyard with barbeque and a swing set, must be the German dream. Tony was out of town, and given what Tony did, Tricia did not know where Tony was or for how long.

The children attended school from eight in the morning to four in the afternoon so between dropping them and picking them up Tricia drove her father around for eight hours either to the City of Frankfurt or to the countryside, that was now brown and partially covered with snow. "It is very beautiful in the Spring and Summer, lots of flowers, you have to come back then." On the evenings John spent as much time with the children as these allowed, but it was not much as they preferred the television and the Internet. On Saturday the four drove to Munich and stayed overnight, did plenty of sightseeing and were back at home on Sunday night. On Monday Patricia took John to walk around Frankfurt. Lots of small talk for seven days but John realized the lack of connection to his daughter and his grandchildren. They had one real conversation about Jack, that was not good by any measure, and John sensed a great deal of resentment in his daughter.

— "You never accepted Jack. You did not know who Jack was and you did not care to know. And when Jack told you about him, you shot him off, you never listened. You and your stupid Irish macho shit. Mom and I always knew about Jack and we loved him the same. You hardly saw any of us, you were always at work or with your men friends, maybe that's the way it is with you policemen." Jack attempted explanations about his work and about how much they needed the overtime money but it did not help. Patricia unloaded what she must have contained for twelve years, her's was a mean uncompassionate speech. "Jack suffered a lot. It's a damn shame what happened to him, Jack deserved better, he did not deserve to die and deserved a father too." At 1035 HS on Tuesday John boarded United's Flight 8836 leaving three strangers behind.

After reading yesterday's New York Times and the latest Newsweek Magazine, John ate his lunch with several glasses of a Pinot Noir from Bordeaux, tried to sleep but couldn't as Patricia had filled him with guilt and decided to read the book Mrs. Petersen had given him, John Grisham's 'The Client'. He figured he had liked the movie, the book should be good. It was not until he finished the fifth chapter and had been up to the lavatory for the second time that John found the sheet of paper folded and inserted between pages in the rear of the book. It was an eight-and-a-half by eleven white computer printout sheet folded in half, some sort of spreadsheet with many lines of numbers that meant nothing to John, dates and figures, accountant stuff. On the back of the sheet, handwritten in black ink, three lines of numbers, the second line subtracted from the top line, the lowest line the difference: 12,234 k. In accountant's parlance that amounts to twelve million two-hundred thirty-four thousand dollars. And below the figures one line of text: 'KEY' in capital letters and next to it an arrow pointing to 'Stephen Vesic'. John had no way to find out if this was a message to him from Mrs. Petersen or if it had been left in the book by Jack. Not been able to recognize Jack's handwriting made John feel ashamed, maybe Patricia's resentment had validity. If it were from Mrs. Petersen it would be logical that she would have pointed to the message in some manner, it was more likely to be from Jack, a note to himself written on the back of a sheet of scrap paper. He would find out before the end of the day.

It was Sergeant Mackenzie that was waiting for him next to a black four-door Ford parked at the curb. John saw Sergeant Mackenzie from a distance through the glass door and kept studying her as the figure grew larger sure that with the glass in between she would not be able to tell. Carol Mackenzie was

25

not too tall and could loose a few pounds, looked tomboyish, brown hair cut short, olive skin, and had an abundance of what men look at. She was wearing a skirt below the knee, looked beige of light gray, and a dark brown sweater. John tried to remember the color of her eyes, green. Good looking young woman, a lot younger than the women John hung around with in Orlando, probably Jack's age. Sergeant Mackenzie had her arms crossed in front of her and some garment folded over her arms, looked black. She was smiling when John came across the glass door, looking better as John got closer, probably because of her skin coloring, or maybe her smile; Sergeant Mackenzie was cute. John was right on the eyes color, light green. For a moment John thought that Sergeant Carol Mackenzie was going to hug him, but she did not.

— "Did you get a good look?" Sergeant Mackenzie opened the trunk for John's one suitcase and carry-on.

— "Meaning, Sergeant Mackenzie?"

— "Meaning me, there is more light inside than outside, I could see you looking straight at me all the time. It's all right John, I dressed for you to look at me." They were in the car, safety belts not yet on. The sweater was navy blue, the tint in the glass had distorted the color, and the folded coat was navy blue as well.

— "If I remember correctly, when I left for Germany I was Lieutenant O'Rourke, now I'm John. What's happened? There are certain courtesies one is expected to keep even with retired lieutenants, actually more with retired lieutenants."

— "No, not in our case. I'm gonna call you John from now on, you better get used to it. And by the way, Captain Kazmierski took Miller off the detail, I'll be your guide and driver."

— "I don't need a guide, I was born and raised in Chicago. I know the town, and you're from out of town."

— "All right then, I'll be your driver." They were leaving the Airport.

— "And on account of what is Sergeant Miller out and young Sergeant Mackenzie has the detail?"

— "I'm older than Miller. On account of two things. On first account, as you will soon find out I'm very smart and a very hard worker and Captain Kazmierski thought that since I'm the guy in charge of crime-scene and you are the superstar who wrote the book, I should stick with you so you can mentor me. Captain Kazmierski thought that was a good move, that the Department will benefit from your expertise, and that maybe I'll update your training manual. On second account, I asked him."

— "You said you're one of the guys. You're not a guy, Sergeant Carol Mackenzie, you are a young woman."

— "And what's wrong with that?"

— "It's the first part, Sergeant Mackenzie, the 'young' part. You are hardly older than my daughter and probably younger than my son. I'm a fifty-four year old man living in Orlando, Florida. Unlike many, I don't fool around with kids."

— "Jack was thirty-one and soon I'll be thirty-five?"

— "How soon?"

— "In twenty-nine months."

— "When I met you first I thought your name sounded familiar, now I'm sure it doesn't."

— "That's one of the two things men say when they meet me."

— "And the other?"

— "The other is a teaser, they ask me if I am Father Mackenzie's daughter. I don't find it funny."

— "That's because you're too young to have a well-developed sense of humor. As you grow up you'll see the humor in much of what you're exposed to. Who's Father Mackenzie?" Carol took her foot off the accelerator and the Ford slowed down. "You don't know who Father Mackenzie is? Now, this is something we're going to work on, we have to. You really don't know who Father Mackenzie is?" Carol turned towards John and made a face to show her incredibility and sang to the tune of 'Eleanor Rigby': "Father Mackenzie writing the words of a sermon that no one will hear, No one comes near." Carol laughed as she changed lanes. "You don't recognize that line?"

— "See what I mean, you're much too young. Now listen, I-am-not-too-old, it's only that you're too young." They were on a ramp leading to the Loop.

— "I'll tell you how we're going to work this out, we're going to date for a while, after that I'm going to marry you and we'll be very happy. But first we

27

have to work on you, you don't remember how to date, you say all the wrong things, you've got to wise up. We'll start tonight, we're going to the movies and after the movie we'll eat Chinese."

— "Carol Mackenzie, you're out of your mind. Don't you have a boyfriend, somebody close to your age? I know a lot about you, I asked Captain Kazmierski too, you seemed too young to be in charge of scene. Gene told me about you."

— "I ditched my boyfriend two days ago, it wasn't hard, for me I mean, I realized I was missing you all the time, so I dropped him. I'm a one-man woman." Carol looked at John and raised her eyebrows. "Listen, I'm still on the clock. Our date starts at six tonight, What do we do before?"

— "Drive to Jack's office. Do you know where it is?"

— "I sure do. And what's this that you know about me? So you like me too."

— "I know a lot about you, except your nickname, but I'll get to that. I know you're single, you come from Philadelphia, you did criminology at Penn State, earned your Master's there. Big deal tennis player they tell me."

— "I played number one singles for Penn State for four years, I was ranked in the top twenty-three in the country in my senior year, I'm still good at it. I'll park on the curb, we'll walk from there."

— "I'll clear your delusions later when we're back in the car. From now on I'm Lieutenant O'Rourke. Capice?"

— "Italians say 'A capito?', 'Capice' does not mean anything. O capito, Lieutenant O'Rourke." There were in front of Jack's building.

— "I remember now. 'Father Mackenzie, Look at him working, darning his socks in the night when there's nobody there, What does he care?... Father Mackenzie, wiping the dirt from his hands as he walks from the grave, No one was saved.' Very poignant words, I don't think you're old enough to capture their meaning. Loneliness is a state of mind, it has nothing to do with how many people are around. " They entered Jack's building. "Now listen up Sergeant, there is a development you don't know of, not yet. Stay with me and keep your mouth shut, all the time, ask me no questions, just listen. You'll understand. I'll show a piece of paper when we're in the elevator."

The elevator stopped at the fancy reception area on the sixth floor. John walked to one of the receptionists, she recognized him. "I remember you Mr. O'Rourke, you're Jack's father, I never had a chance to tell you how sorry I am. Jack was wonderful." She smiled and waited for John to acknowledge. "Are you coming to see Mr. DeSimone? He has somebody with him now."

— "Actually no, I brought some chocolates from Germany for Mrs. Peterson. Can she come here?"

— "Of course, I'll ring her." It took Mrs. Peterson no more that three minutes, she probably jogged.

— "I'm so happy to see you. Are you here to get your paintings? They're wrapped waiting in Jack's office."

— "Yes, that's right. But I brought you Swiss chocolates from Germany, you'll love them. I had to leave the chocolates downstairs, at the security desk. Do you want to come down with us to fetch them?"

The three walked to the Starbucks across LaSalle Street. "I have something to show you. Let's order and sit first, I don't want to be too obvious." They took their coffees to a table away from the window. "I found your message in Jack's book but I could not make up what it means. You'll have to help me out." John passed the book to Mrs. Peterson and pulled the folded paper from the book.

— "It's not my message. The paper was there, it's a marker for the last page you read. The handwriting is Jack's, that I'm sure of. He left the marker there in the book and I saved it. Do you think it's important?"

— "Mrs. Peterson, in my line of work everything is important until proven otherwise, and even if something at first does not seem relevant it is still kept because its relevance may be discovered later. We turn every stone. I believe this sheet is relevant, it's about twelve million two-hundred thirty-four thousand dollars relevant; this may have to do with what you told me about somebody robbing these people blind, that may be Jack's account of the amount. What do you think?"

— "I can't tell, it's a number that Jack wrote down. He never said anything to me." Mrs. Peterson's coffee was too hot.

— "And the name? Jack gave a key to Stephen Vesic, or maybe Stephen Vesic gave the key to Jack. The key to what? Can you help me here? Is there a locker, a box, anything you may think of? You worked with Jack, Did he mention this Stephen Vesic to you?"

29

— "I don't know what you mean by mention. Jack never told me anything about Vesic, but he asked me to find out Vesic's address. I remember that. It wasn't easy but I did."

— "Jack asked for Vesic's address, not his telephone number?"

— "That's right, but I got Jack both, took me a while, but I found both."

— "How did you find out?"

— "Vesic is not in the telephone book. There are Vesic's but no Stephen. I called UPS, FedEx and other carriers we use and none has a record. I checked surrounding areas, no dice. I found Vesic calling Cook County's office of licenses. They found him in their database, he had acquired a license for his firm, something or rather export-import near the port. I gave the address and phone number to Jack and he asked me to write a label for a FedEx envelope."

— "Do you have Vesic's address?"

— "No, I gave it to Jack but I'm sure I can find it again, all I have to do is locate the FedEx charge in our record, I'll do that as soon as we go back, it won't take a minute."

— "You do that. Give the address to Sergeant Mackenzie, she'll stay with you. I'll go back to get the frames and I'll see DeSimone, he may know about Vesic. You're sure Vesic is not an accountant in the firm?"

— "I'm positive. I'll find Vesic's address for you." Mrs. Peterson ate her biscotto and finished her coffee. "You said something about chocolates."

— "Sergeant, please walk back to the car and find a box of chocolates in my handbag. I'm sure you don't mind."

— "I'll be back in a minute, Lieutenant O'Rourke sir."

John had to wait more than twenty minutes for DeSimone to finish his meeting. In the meantime he received the customary ice-cold bottles of flavored tea and water, and shared the tea with Carol. Mrs. Peterson went to her desk and returned with Vesic's address before DeSimone showed up looking sharp in a blue blazer with brass buttons and gray flannel pants.

— "If you're coming for the paintings, I have them ready to go in Jack's office. Come walk with me, maybe I'll calm down."

— "What's the matter?"

Jack's office was empty except for the Modigliani frames wrapped in bubble plastic leaning on a wall. "Let me tell you something that may help you understand Jack. Just now I met with two potential clients, middle-management stiffs at a large hospital, to see if we can help them straighten out their show, and had to put up with condescension that I don't deserve, I earned an MBA at Kellogg for heaven's sake. Someone must have forewarned these two bozos of my homosexuality so they were tiptoing around words and talked to me as if I were some flower girl, careful about what they said and how they said it. I bench-press one-hundred and fifty pounds, seven pounds over my weight, and I've been training in martial arts since I was twelve, that's more years than you need to know. I felt like throwing both of them off the window but I have to be composed because they are potential clients. You know Christian is…, was, a martial arts instructor, ranked in Illinois. And I'm sure that he and Jack had to put up with the same crap. I'll make us two espressi." DeSimone turned to the shiny chrome coffee maker.

— "I need to ask you something. Do you know a man by the name of Stephen Vesic, has an import-export firm here in Chicago. Maybe a client? Maybe Vesic works for your firm?"

— "I'm sure I don't know any Vesic, it's an important part of my job to remember names, faces too. Let me check the database and see if he is or was a client. The database goes back to client one, names can not be ever erased." DeSimone walked outside to his secretary's desk and returned after a few minutes. "Nobody of that last name or similar names starting with small ve or be, It is small ve, isn't it?" John nodded. The coffee was ready and DeSimone served from the chrome containers into two porcelain cups, white with tiny gold stars. The contraption made good coffee. "Where did you get the name? What's with it?"

John had decided it was best to share his finding with DeSimone. "I found this sheet folded inside one of Jack's books, there is a note Jack wrote on the back of scrap paper. Here, look it over."

— "Inside a book you said. One of our books? Here?"

— "No, a novel, one of Jack's books." No need to reveal more.

— "In Jack's house?"

— "Can't disclose that."

— "If you look at the spreadsheet's upper right corner you'll see the date it was printed. It is the Friday before Jack's passing." John cursed himself for not noticing the date. "That means that Jack wrote the note between that Friday and the following Monday." Not bad for Mister MBA from Kellogg.

— "Can you think what the key could have been for? Are there lockers here? A strong box? We don't know if Jack received the key from Vesic or if he was giving Vesic the key."

— "There are no lockers in our offices. We have several strong boxes, Jack had no access to any, nor do I for that matter." DeSimone did not comment about the three lines of figures. "The direction of the key suggests that Jack gave the key to Vesic, not the other way around."

— "Not necessarily, Jack may have received the key from Vesic and wrote a note to himself that he had to return it." Sergeant Mackenzie walked into the office and introduced herself to DeSimone. "Did you say Mackenzie, the name sounds familiar. We haven't met, have we?"

Jack waited at the curb with the frames while Carol went for the car. "I don't know where the street is, we have to find out how to get to Vesic's place."

— "I know where it is. Mrs. Peterson printed a map for me from the Internet. She's sweet, she told me I should marry you. She's smart too."

— "Listen Sergeant, I may have to get rough with Vesic. I will if I need to. I'm armed. If I confirm this fellow killed my son I'm not planning to make an arrest, if you follow me. I'd rather you stay out of the way, I don't want to place you in danger or to get you in trouble with the department. You'll stay in the car. It doesn't look like you're armed."

— "Staying in the car is not approved procedure, we'll be safer together, separated we're both exposed. Yes, I'm armed, nine millimeter, fourteen rounds in the clip, I carry an extra clip."

— "And where do you carry all that iron?"

— "That, John, you'll find out only after our fifth date, I'm an old-fashioned girl from Philadelphia."

Vesic's building was an unattractive two-story brick structure with an unremarkable entrance and few small windows. It had 'cheap rent' written all over. The directory in the lobby did not list the Buckingham Import-Export Company. A young man dressed in a warm-up suit and wearing a set of earphones had his face six inches in front of a laptop's screen. "We're looking for Steve Vesic of Buckingham Import-Export Company."

— "He's not here." The young fellow never took his eyes off the screen.

— "How can you know if you haven't checked it?" He kept his eyes on the screen.

— "Because they're never here. Not once in the year and a half I've worked in this rat hole. Once in a while they receive an overnight parcel and it's gone next morning, they pick them up during the night. They have a key. There is no night attendant." Never moved his face from the screen. "If you ask me it's cocaine they import. I suppose so long as they pay the rent nobody gives a shit."

— "Take us there."

— "No way, José." Now the young man looked up, he was cross-eyed. "Nobody goes nowhere unless it is the tenant or my boss says so. And my boss ain't here." Michael placed his unfolded wallet between the young man's face and the laptop's screen to show his detective's gold badge. "Chicago Police Department. We have reason to believe these people are implicated in the murder of two men here in Chicago. Take us to the office, now!" The young man was very short.

— "You mean the two queer." John showed his character and restraint by not pressing the young man's face inward.

— "No, I mean the two men, move your ass or I'll drag you there. You'll stay in the office with us, I don't want you making phone calls to nofuckingbody." Not so much restraint now. "Open the door and walk inside. Don't touch anything." John opened his jacket to let his semi-automatic pistol show. Stand where you are and keep your hands where I see them, don't do anything stupid." The furniture consisted of a wood desk, three chrome chairs, a non-matching credenza and a metal file cabinet with four drawers. There was plenty of dust on every surface. John opened all the drawers in the desk and the credenza, a few sheets of blank paper, office supplies, electric bulbs, a half-full box of gummy bears, a fifty-foot tape measure. No receipts, no paid bills, no Rolodex, no telephone. In the file cabinet there were no files, only a wood box containing a chess set, not a fancy set but a classic set with large wood men. John used his handkerchief to lift several men, the varnish was worn in the middle and in the top. "Whomever owns this set is a serious player, the varnish is actually worn out in the top, you can see the duller shin, this set belongs to someone who plays frequently." John put the chess set back where he found it. "There is nothing here Sergeant." John turned to face the young man. "Listen up, keep all of this to yourself, we'll have four plain-clothes officers twenty-four-seven watching all entrances, we want to catch these guys. Make sure you don't scare them away, you'll be in deep shit if you do. A capito?" John winked to Carol.

John had the feeling he forgot something or that there was something he saw that did not register. Maybe it will come back. "I need to think. Drive anywhere you want to, go west, don't talk to me, I have to place all this stuff in order." Ten minutes passed, they were on Cermak Street going west. Carol drove slow, she didn't want to find herself in Iowa before John spoke. It was ten past seven, a little early for dinner but not too early. Fifteen minutes later John spoke, they were west of West Chester. "Where the hell are we? Why did you drive this far?"

— "You said to drive west, that's what I did. Where did I go wrong?" John gave her a look that would kill a pigeon.

— "Turn around, we're going back to Old Town, I'm taking you to eat goulash? Do you like goulash?"

— "Yes I do, goody-goody, I like dumplings too. They're not good for my figure but I'll run two miles tomorrow before I pick you up. I mean before I go to your brother's house for you, I already picked you up."

— "How do you now about my brother? Were you at Patrick's house?"

— "I found out, I'm a detective. I met your brother at the Green Dandy Pub, and his wife too, I think I made a good impression. Where in Old Town?"

— "Keep going straight, we'll turn left soon. I hope the joint is still there."

— "So-o-o, How am I doing so far, lieutenant? I'm not learning that much, I don't think. But it's fun, I enjoy being with you. You know I found out your nickname, you have two actually, from the old days I mean. One is long."

— "Listen, Sergeant, you're getting out of hand, let's keep rank in the picture."

— "No-o-o, it's past seven, I'm off the clock. We're having our first date and you're taking me for goulash and dumplings. We'll go to the same place every year, it'll be so romantic. Are you having a good time?"

— "What's with the nickname?"

— "The guys called you 'Attention to Detail', A-T-D for short."

— "And the other one?"

— "Fastidious." It sounds to me like you were a pain in the butt. And I noticed earlier that you use colorful language too. Another facet of your complex personality, that's what attracted me to you."

— "Turn left, we're going to the Restaurant Budapest, middle of the block, drop me at the door, you go find a parking spot. What did you say your handle is?"

— "Clue Finder, I have it on my license plate."

— "Not possible, two letters too many."

— "I took the 'Es' out."

— "That's your Internet handle, I mean your nickname in the Department."

— "Don't have one. Get out of the car. Get a good table. Red wine."

— "I have better dates in Orlando. So far, this is our first date and you're nagging me. Such doesn't happen to me in Orlando."

John was on the first page of the wine list when Carol reached the table, hardly two minutes after he had sat down. "How did you get here so fast?"

— "I parked at the fire hydrant, I'm a police-woman."

Carol was a good eater. They had goulash and dumplings and drank Hungarian wine, and sheared vanilla ice cream for dessert. "We're going to walk a couple of blocks to a place I know."

— "A hotel? The answer is no can do. This is our first date, we're only beginning to know each other. You're too audacious, Fastidious." John gave Carol a stern look.

— "A chess club, it's called The Chess Club."

The Chess Club consisted of two rooms connected by a double door that has never been closed, both rooms filled with small square tables each with two Vienna chairs on opposite sides, two bathrooms that only men use and a broom closet. Not what you would call fancy. Smokey, dusty wood floors with stepped-on cigarette butts everywhere, walls last painted during the Truman administration, ceiling fans that did not work and a heating system that occasionally comes to life. It is the hang out of many of the better chess players in Chicago, lots of Central Europeans with a sprinkle of Cubans, Spaniards and Americans. There were men playing in more than half of the tables, all with timing devices, men standing up next to certain tables, arms crossed on their chests and serious looks on their faces. Carol waited on the street. John approached the man sitting at the desk and said he was looking for Vladimir Vesic.

— "Vladimir Vesic, no Vladimir Vesic, only Vesic I know is Bobby Vesic, he no play here, not fancy enough for Bobby, never play here, Vesic good player, a prick but good player, he plays at The Radeski Club on Wells Street, ten blocks from here."

— "The Radeski Club, I don't think so, and the name is Vladimir, everybody calls him Vlad, likes to drink Cognac."

— "No, this Vesic drinks nothing but Slivovitz, no Cognac, Vesic is no Vladimir, maybe Stefan but no Vladimir, all call him Bobby for Bobby Fisher. Good player this Vesic, a prick but good player." John tipped the man a twenty-dollar bill to prove he was not a prick like Vesic and walked outside.

— "We need to find a liquor store. I have our man. Walk with me."

— "You gave the old lady Swiss chocolates and I get liquor. You're not being romantic, John."

John spent ninety-six dollars on a bottle of the best Slivovitz they had in stock and returned the bottle to the red cardboard case with raised silver letters and bought a large white bow that he attached to the front of the case. They walked three blocks to The Radeski Club.

— "You walk in there and tell the attendant you have a bottle of Slivovitz for Bobby Vesic. Wait to see that the attendant gives the bottle to Vesic and walk outside. I'll take it from there, you point Vesic to me."

— "And if Vesic isn't there?"

— "Leave the case, don't ask questions, see that the case is placed where we can see it from the street."

— "Will do." Carol walked into the Radeski Club, kept her eyes fixed on the man in front of the coat room and waited until this finished his phone call to hand him the case. The man was speaking a foreign language Carol did not recognize. She chatted a bit and signaled to a shelf and the man placed the case on the shelf. John could see the white bow from across the street.

— "Now we wait. We'll move to the corner and when somebody goes in we walk across and check if the bottle is on the shelf. Go get the car and park it closer. Do you carry a cellular? Give me your number."

— "I already have your number in my cell, I'll call you as I walk. The man at the desk told me that Vesic, he called him Bobby, comes on Friday nights, sometimes Saturday nights and Sunday afternoons, rarely other nights. Today is Tuesday. I didn't ask, he volunteered." Carol was back with the car in thirty minutes. "I telephoned the club. They close at two and open at ten in the morning."

The two alternated making passes every time someone walked in. The white bow remained in place. At twelve-ten one car parked across the street from the club left and they took the parking slot. It was two-twenty when the lights went off in the Radeski Club. "Drop me at my apartment and take the car with you."

— "I'll come for you at eleven and will go for lunch. After lunch we go watch the club until Vesic shows up. Have you done surveillance work?"

— "Not much. I'm on the brains end of the business."

— "Did you say that your father is a farmer and grows smart-asses?"

— "My father is actually a baker in Philadelphia."

— "And how old did you say he is?"

— "Quite older than you. I have three brothers, my parents wanted a girl and kept trying until I showed up. I'm the youngest. My mother knows about you, she liked what I told her."

— "Mackenzie, you're hopeless. Tomorrow you'll bring three coats and hats if you have any. We want to change our appearance not to be obvious."

— "I gathered that, I've been on the force for several years. I'll see you in the morning. Sleep well.

CHAPTER 5
CHECK MATE

CAROL HAD COLLECTED TWO ski jackets, one light blue, the other black, a raincoat and a navy blue trench coat and she brought half a dozen ski caps. John had a raincoat too, the black top coat he had bought before flying to Germany and two jackets he borrowed from Patrick. Two hats. For two days they parked their car on lateral streets and changed coats and hats for every trip they took to the front door of The Radeski Club, taking turns. Early evening and near midnight they ate pizza and drank sodas. The white bow was visible from the street, Vesic never showed up. On Friday they did the same routine with the same clothes. At 2120 HS the white bow was not there. John waited ten minutes before entering the place.

— "Say, I'm looking for Bobby Vesic, I sent him a bottle earlier."

— "So it was from you, You looking to play Bobby? He's got a game already, he's always booked, maybe next Friday." The attendant had what John correctly took for a Hungarian accent.

— "Do you mind asking him?"

— "Not during a game. It'll be half an hour, maybe forty minutes, they are playing thirty seconds. You know is one-hundred a game, three games, Bobby won't play for less and he don't take no cards."

— "I play for three hundred a game, three games. Go tell Bobby."

— "I'll need to see your cash. The table will cost you forty, Bobby don't pay. You may sit at the bar but don't go to the table, nobody knows you, they don't

38

like strangers. Go have a drink." John nodded and showed the man several hundred-dollar bills."

— "I have to keep the money first and then I'll ask Bobby. He breaks for drink when he finishes." John gave the man nine hundred-dollar bills and four twenties.

— "Forty for you. I'll watch from the bar."

The Radeski Club was one large rectangular room with thirty-eight, John counted them, square tables, two Vienna chairs to a table just like at The Chess Club, the floor was wood parquet, waxed, no cigarette butts, the walls were lined with framed photographs of notable chess players and celebrated locals. John had not known this place. There was a bar with nine stools on the right side, two men at the bar, one bartender that moved at a snail pace. The coat room was a recess in the wall, probably a closet that had been opened up, one rack with many coats, all black or near black, many hats on two shelves. In front of the coat room a counter, two old-style telephones on it, a door on one side of the counter, maybe a closet, maybe the manager's office. In the back of the room, next to the end of the bar a door with a sign that read bathrooms. John ordered a beer and walked to use the men's bathroom, it has a window to a back alley but with steel bars, no way for anybody to leave through the bars, not even a child. John checked the lady's room, no window.

John's beer was waiting at the end of the bar, tall glass with a German name etched on it, ice-cold, the right amount of foam, the bartender was old and slow but knew how to throw a beer. John placed a twenty dollar bill on the counter and sat on a stool with his back leaning on the bar. There were games going at one-third of the tables but the attention was on one table in the center of the room, surrounded by men all in dark suits that followed the game and hid the players from John's view. John imagined Vesic to be one of the two players at that table.

Carol was sitting inside the Ford, parked directly across the entrance door to The Radeski Club. Two men in black overcoats were standing in front of one of the windows looking inside, not together but one at each end of the window, both of them had their hands in their coat pockets, a cold Chicago night. Carol did not make anything of it. John had said to wait in the car and to watch if Vesic left with the Slivovitz case, and to follow him on foot.

At forty minutes after ten the group watching the game started applauding and kept it up for almost a minute before they dispersed to other tables and to the bar. The players stood up, one was a thin man in a black suit that looked no different that the spectators, the other more robust with very long dark wavy hair, dressed in a gray tweed jacket and a wide orangy red tie. The body language told John that the one in the tweed jacket had taken the pot and he figured this to be Vesic. The two players stayed at the table for a few minutes, chatting, the one in the black suit stood up first and walked to the bar. The one in the tweed jacket remained at the table, several of the spectators came to shake his hand. The attendant joined the group and bent to the one in the tweed jacket's ear. This stood up, the attendant pointed at John, they spoke a few words and the one in the tweed jacket walked towards the bar, in a straight line to John, smiling all the time as people touched him, and shook hands with two. From the car Carol could see John sitting at the bar and a man walking towards him. She did not take notice that one of the two men standing by the window had walked away.

Vesic stood in front of John and grabbed John's right hand with his two hands and shook it vigorously, standing very close to John and smiling widely. Good looking man, mid-fiftish, as tall as John, under two-hundred pounds, narrow shoulders, with the sort of deep bronze tan one sees more in Orlando than in Chicago, bright black eyes, very long wavy black hair that hid large ears, not a speck of white. The orangy tie seemed out of place, too flashy.

— "You want to play me? Where did you say you're from?" Vesic had an accent that John could not make. He acted very friendly.

— "Orlando, Florida."

— "Lovely place, I've been to Disney's many times, best place in America after Las Vegas. And I thank you for the bottle, good choice, best drink ever made." Vesic knocked twice on the counter to get the bartender's attention, and this soon brought Vesic his usual Slivovitz in a crystal glass different to those everybody else had. No question Vesic was a celebrity in The Radeski Club. Vesic took a small sip and raised his eyebrows as if he were surprised. "I don't see why I shouldn't play you. If you win you'll have many fans here, but you have to win first. I say two out of three, winner takes all. Thirty seconds all right with you?" Humility was not one of Vesic's virtues.

— "Truth is I'm not sure I want to be shamed in front of all these people, I haven't played chess since high school and it's been a while. I only want to talk to you, I'm willing to pay, I need to have the key back." John sipped his beer to give Vesic time to answer.

— "The key?"

— "The key. Jack O'Rourke's key. The key Jack gave you."

— "I have no key. I'm afraid you have me confused. I never heard of that person. I don't know what you're talking about. Are you saying you don't want to play me?" What are you? A comedian? Who are you?"

— "That's too many questions. Listen, I don't want no quarrel with you, but I've got to have the key. Now. If I don't walk out of this place with the key in my hand, you and me are gonna be in a bat of shit. Trust me on that. If O'Rourke owes you money, we'll pay you, but I need the key, now." John stressed 'we'.

The attendant touched Vesic's shoulder. "You have a phone call. From Europe. At the desk."

— "Listen, I have to take this call, my cellular does not reach the continent. Business. Please stay here, I'm sure we'll straighten this out." Vesic seemed sincere but just the same John stood up and kept his eyes on him. The desk was no more than forty feet away. If Vesic attempted to take off John would reach him before he could get to the door leading to the street.

Vesic took the call leaning on the desk and soon he moved to the other side of the desk. The voice spoke Serbian. "Don't talk, just listen and do as I say, you're compromised. Say you understand."

— "I do." Serbian.

— "You have to go home. Not tomorrow, now, this minute. Do you have what you need?"

— "No, I need to go to my apartment."

— "What did the man ask you?"

— "He wants a key. I have no key. I know nothing about a key."

— "Anything else?"

— "No, just the key."

— "You are sure? Nothing else?"

— "Nothing else, just the key. I'm sure."

— "Good. In that case you'll be able to come back soon."

— "Weeks?"

— "Weeks."

— "Anything else?"

— "No, go home. I'll telephone Novak. Make sure you stay on your route. Don't meet anybody, no whoring, no conversations. You've been indiscreet. Don't spend more than minutes at your apartment. Take no more than what you're supposed to take."

— "Everything is ready. I'll be careful. I always am." Vesic had turned his back to John and was facing the door that led to Boris's office. There was silence on the line. Vesic continued speaking Serbian and paced the floor behind the desk going back and forth twice as John watched him. On the next turn, as he reached the door to the manager's office, Vesic dropped the phone and rushed through the door, locking it from the other side. He reached the alley through the back door and ran to Wieland Street, kept running being careful of staying away from the curb, turned on Schiller and then onto Park Avenue and kept the same fast pace for two blocks until he arrived at his apartment building on Evergreen Avenue. Vesic did not go into his apartment, he walked the stairs one floor down to the garage, the documents and everything else he would need were in the leather bag in the trunk of his Toyota Camry. Vesic pulled out of the garage, drove towards Interstate 80 and was on his way to St. Louis, Missouri, by the time John and Carol were convinced they had lost him. Too bad for the nine hundred dollars, small sum but he liked making money playing chess.

— "We lost him. We lost him. He tricked me. He pretended to have a phone call and shook me. Shit. I should have told Gene and he'd have somebody watching the rear. Damn it, I blew it." Let's go back to the club. They had lost the parking slot, so Carol double-parked. A patrol car showed up and Carol showed the officer her badge.

— "Give me the nine-hundred-eighty. Say one fucking word and you'll loose your face. What's your name?"

— "Alex, my uncle owns the club. I did nothing wrong."

— "Show me the office." As soon as they walked in John pushed Alex against the wall, grabbed his neck with his left hand and opened his coat for Alex to see his weapon. "Listen good, I don't have to kill you but I will if you lie to me." Alex started to sob. "When did Vesic tell you to call him to the phone?"

John pulled his semiautomatic, cocked it and pressed the barrel on Alex's forehead. "Lie to me and I'll kill you right here."

— "He didn't. Somebody called and said it was for Mr. Vesic and that it was from Europe, to get him right away." I did nothing wrong, I only told Bobby. He was happy he was going to take nine hundred dollars from you, you don't look like no player. Bobby said he'd give me a good tip."

— "Give me my fucking money." Alex straightened himself up to pull the bills from his pocket and John noticed that Alex's pants were soaked, Alex had peed on himself. "You say a word, you talk to the cops and I'll come back to kill you. You got that?"

— "I haven't done anything to you, What do you want? Why are you so angry with me?"

— "I want you to keep you trap shot and to watch for Vesic. I'll call you from time to time and you'll tell me when he's back. You fuck up and you'll be sorry. Stay here for a while." Alex was going nowhere until his pants dried out. John walked along the big room walls until he found a frame with Vesic's photograph and took it with him.

Vesic crossed the Mississippi River on Interstate 270 and drove to the town of Hazelwood. He was supposed to have made a dry run months before but he had not and had to spend some time finding a motel with rooms opening to the outside so he would be seen only at the time of checking in. Vesic wore a ski cap to hide his long hair, the tweed jacket he had dropped in a trash can along the way. He was wearing a worn out navy blue zip-up jacket with the Cardinals logo he had bought at a second hand shop together with most of the stuff he carried in the bag. Vesic hated to dress in shabby clothes and could not wait to be in Europe, he would buy the sort of clothes he liked in Paris. He stretched the plastic sheet on the sink and used scissors to cut his hair to just over an inch, doing the best he could in the back. He folded the plastic sheet and placed it in the paper bag he would dispose of before reaching St. Louis, and collected hairs from the sink and floor with a wet towel that he took with him. Vesic did not sleep but laid down for two hours to rest his body. At ten in the morning Vesic drove to Lambert - St. Louis International Airport, parked the Toyota in the long-term parking, collected his belongings, dropped the plastic gloves and the map in a trash container, walked to the arrivals area and rode a cab to downtown St. Louis. The barber asked Vesic where he got such awful hair cut and gave him a short cut that made him look years older. The five-hour bus ride to Branson, Missouri, with all the tourist was fun. After dinner he bought a bus ticket to Little Rock, Arkansas, and the four-hour ride was long enough to catch up with his sleep. Vesic bought a vacation package to take him to Mexico City first and then to Cancun and flew Delta. In Mexico City he bought his ticket to Frankfurt using a passport that showed his long hair but raised no questions, and arrived in Frankfurt on time for breakfast. Vesic rode the TGV to Paris, spent a day shopping for clothes and rode the TGV to Lyon. Two taxi rides took Vesic to his house in the small town of Les Deux Colombes, sixty kilometers north of Marseilles.

Vesic was surprised to see smoke coming out from one of the three chimneys; he had left the house with all windows secured and the doors locked. He asked the taxi driver to wait until he checked the house. The front door was unlocked and there was a smell of food being cooked. Vesic found Vlad in the kitchen and gave him a big hug. "Wait until I send the cab off. I'm glad you're here. You're looking old for a kid your age." They spoke Serbian. Vesic gave the cab driver a ten-Euro tip for his troubles.

— "Novak sent me over. He's worried about you, you're a day late. I'll call him to let him know. Ready to eat? I cooked a fat rabbit and potatoes. And made a soup. Have some wine here?"

Vesic pulled two bottles of Cabernet Sauvignon from the cabinet and went upstairs for a bottle of Slivovitz that he placed in the freezer. Both the freezer and the refrigerator were empty but there was plenty of ice. "You've been here for a while? The freezer is cold."

— "Since yesterday morning, Novak sent me to wait for you. He wants both of us in Marseille tomorrow night. I brought a seven-hundred that I'm supposed to leave with you later, it's in the barn. Novak treats you better than me and I'm Novak's nephew, not fair." They both laughed.

It was three in the afternoon by the time they finished the rabbit and one and one-half bottles of Cabernet, they sat on the big sofa by the fire and ate figs and cheeses for dessert and drank Slivovitz until the early evening. "I'll call Novak, you pour me more of that plum wine of yours." Vlad listened for two minutes and passed the telephone to Vesic.

— "You're a day late Stefan. A day late and you were told not to be late, you were told to follow instructions and you didn't. And you were indiscrete in America too. You may jeopardize our work, you're not responsible as you used to be. You used to be a good man but your stupid chess playing got to your head. You want to be seen and your job is to be invisible, you'll be punished." Novak did not give Vesic a chance to reply, he terminated the call. Vesic shrugged his shoulders and turned to Vlad. "He's mad at me again. I think it's that time of the month." Vesic thought he was being funny but Vlad did not, he laughed only to make Vesic feel at ease, but only a short laugh. Vesic had his back to the fire and was facing Vlad, who was standing with both arms behind his back and facing Vesic, twenty feet away. "What, Are you mad at me too?, What's the big deal? What's with you people? Can't I have a little fun to go with the hard work?"

Vlad walked towards Vesic and extended both arms in front of him, in his left hand Vlad was holding a 22-caliber Smith & Wesson revolver with a noise-suppressor at the end of its long barrel. He shot twice when he was eight feet in front of Vesic and placed both slugs in Vesic's heart. 'You have to be accurate with small caliber, any clown can kill you with a forty-five. A twenty-two requires talent and precision.' Vlad bent forward and placed the end of the silencer on Vesic's forehead. Novak had said four in the head, two to do the job and two for being indiscreet. "I forgot to tell you, Novak said to let you know he's sorry. Me too." That was the end of the easy part. Tomorrow he will have to dig a grave inside the barn and will have to fill it too. Vlad decided he would take all the wine bottles he could fit in the trunk and in the rear seat, but he would not tell Uncle Novak. Novak did not know what having fun was.

It was very cold in Chicago, the playoffs were on and the Bears were not in. John was able to buy two good tickets for a Bull's game next week, that will be date number two. Vesic's photograph had been distributed throughout Illinois as a person of interest in Jack's and Christian's murders. Other than that, the photographs taken at the Green Dandy Pub had been matched with names, telephone. Bank and e-mail records had been received and a team of people had pieced out Jack's and Christian's activities during their last weeks. Nothing extraordinary, they went to work, sometimes on Saturday mornings, ate out, shopped, went to two Bull's games, gave a dinner party at home on a Thursday night, paid bills, went to the gym frequently and twice to the movies on Sunday afternoons. Many detectives had invested many hours for information that did not lead anywhere, but that is always the case until a break happens. The tape showing Jack leaving his office was received from the security company but its format did not fit any of the machines and could not be viewed. All had forgotten about it until John asked to see it. Captain Kazmierski raised hell when he found out and Sergeant Mackenzie said she would call the security company to ask for one in a different format.

— "I appreciate you letting us come here. Start the tape but show us how to stop and rewind, just in case. You don't have to stay, we'll manage. Just the same the department wants a copy in a format we can read. Please talk to Margo in the IT section, she'll let you know what we've got there."

The first part of the tape had six still shots of Jack in the elevator. Elevators cameras do not record continuously but shoot a frame every ten seconds. There were three people in the elevator when Jack got in on the sixth floor, one man, two women. In the last five shots Jack was leaning on the back wall holding his bag in front of him, arms crossed in front of the bag as if protecting it. Two men got on at the third floor and a woman at the second. Everybody faced the door. A camera taped Jack coming out of the elevator with his bag hanging from his right shoulder, another camera had ten seconds of Jack across the lobby and a second camera captured Jack moving his bag to his left shoulder. Jack's was last seen getting to the entrance steps. "Let's look at each face in the elevator and in the lobby, we want to see if anybody followed Jack, talked to Jack and if there is anybody we know." Nobody they knew, nobody appeared to follow Jack. "We'll have Margo print photographs of everybody, we'll identify those we can and we'll interview each to find out if they saw anything." John stood up. "I'm going to the bathroom and will come back with coffee, Want anything else?" No answer, Carol seemed upset. "Now, listen up Sergeant Mackenzie, watch that tape again and tell me what you see. I'll be back in five."

— "I don't need to watch again, I saw it too. The bag, that bag was heavy. The same bag was hanging from a chair in Jack's house, we photographed it. I remember it was empty. We need to go to Jack's house, I'll have to draft an order and we'll need a team to go with us. Can't be just us."

— "Good work, Sergeant. The Captain is right, you're good."

CHAPTER 6
CHUNKY

— "You should have told me John, the deal was that you participate but you don't keep anything to yourself. You placed Sergeant Mackenzie in a bad spot. Unlike you, Sergeant Mackenzie has no choices, she has to tell me of any developments. She'll be reprimanded. I would have put two men in the alley and Vesic would be sitting next to us. We lost the opportunity, you did."

— "I'm sorry Gene. I really am."

— "No, you're not, you were always like that John, you want to do it alone. It has to be a team effort. Now I had to put four men digging into Vesic's life. They'll locate him but it's a waste of at least a hundred hours of taxpayers's money. Now get out of here, Mackenzie and two other people are waiting for you in the car."

Sergeant Mackenzie was in the passenger's seat and Sergeant Miller was at the wheel. Bull Croce was in the back seat. Lieutenant Croce was a fifteen-year man, had played football for the Illini, defensive tackle.

— "Johnny."

— "Bull."

Miller drove to Jack's house, Bull Croce photographed Carol as she cut the seals. Jack's bag was where it was supposed to be, hanging from one of the chairs in the first floor office. A black leather portfolio with a zipper on three sides that when unzipped opens up like a book. One interior pocket with a zipper. Nothing in the bag. Several photographs were taken, their purpose to document that the bag was empty. Bull Croce said they were trying to prove a negative. John treated the group for lunch at Uno. Carol's cellular rang during her second slice of Sicilian. "It's for you, Captain Kazmierski."

— "Gene."

— "You're in luck, it did not take a hundred hours. Vesic popped up in the Michigan database, he has an export license and works out of Muskegon, Michigan. Ships parts for old cars to France, port of entry Marseille. No priors except two misdemeanors, he was caught twice gambling in the same parlor, paid the fines and walked. We placed several alerts, he'll pop up soon enough, we'll have to go Michigan to interview him."

— "Great, thanks Gene. We'll all be back at the station in a couple of hours."

The real break came on Wednesday, minutes past two in the morning. The company that installed and services the alarm system in Jack's house called the officer on duty to report someone inside the house using an outdated password. A black-and-white with two officers was on the scene within minutes; a second unit arrived minutes later. Four officers entered the house with vests on and weapons drawn. The officers turned all lights on as they moved in. One officer remained on the first floor, two went upstairs and the fourth descended to the basement. Nobody in the upper floors. Nobody in the first floor. In the basement the lights were on; the metal cabinet with the four lockers had been swung forward and there was light behind it. The officer waited for the other three to join him before swinging the metal cabinet all the way out.

Two officers went through the opening. Inside they saw what looked like a small forest, a large space crammed with tables supporting wood boxes filled with dirt and marihuana plants. The lights hanging from the ceiling were very bright, there were rubber hoses on the tables, water dripping here and there, garden tools on the tables. To the left of the opening, a man in a dark green warm up suit was leaning on a table with both hands on the table's edge. In front of the man, a pile of small packages and a black backpack.

— "Who else is here?" No answer. The man looked at the floor. "Keep him covered, I'll check. If he takes his hands off the table shoot both legs. Don't fuck with us buddy." It took a few minutes to verify there was nobody else in the basement.

— "Listen up, keep both hands on the edge and move your feet away from the table. More. Lean forward. More." Officer Spencer kept his 45-caliber 1911 Colt semi-automatic trained on the man's side, Peterson moved behind the man to frisk him and handcuff the man's hands behind his back. In his pants pocket the man carried folded dollar bills and a set of car keys, no identification. Hanging from a plastic string around his neck a key; later on it turned out to be the key to Jack's house. Peterson read the man his rights, "You have the right to remain silent", and so on.

— "Kneel on the floor. What are you doing here?" No answer, the man kept staring at the floor. The officer grabbed the man's shirt collar behind his back and pushed forward while holding the shirt collar not to have to explain a broken nose, then he tied the man's ankles with a plastic strap. "He ain't going nowhere. Take these keys, call for the wrecker to come impound his car. Walk around and use the clicker, can't be too far, the car lights will go on. Call the dispatcher and get Captain Kazmierski's cellular. Ask the Captain to meet us here."

The backpack was empty. On the table they counted twenty-four bricks. In two sets of adjacent open shelves they counted six-hundred plus marihuana bricks. One of the officers walked back and forth and attempted to count the plants and stopped at one-hundred-fifty having counted fewer than half. The rubber hoses on the tables were connected to manifolds and some leaked on the floor. There were fire sprinklers attached to pipes on the ceiling. The officer did not find heaters but the room was hot, probably form the overhead lights. Near the entrance, on the side opposite the shelving with the bricks, two trash compactors of the type used to pack cardboard, with plastic bags half-full with dry leaves and twigs. Vents and large exhaust fans were discovered later in the rear of the room.

Captain Kazmierski took the call on his cellular at 0255 HS and immediately called John, told him what happened and said he'd pick him up. They arrived at Jack's house before four. The intruder already had been taken to the police station to be booked for breaking an entry and attempted robbery. His car was towed to the police garage to be inspected. "Holy mackerel Johnny, this is an industrial operation, it'll break fifty state and federal laws, if not more. The State will want to impound the house, I don't think you'll find a way to stop them. Did you know about this? Of course you don't." John walked around to size the place and counted the number of bricks on the shelves.

— "There is over a quarter of a million dollars in weed bricks here. The plants will yield as much. I could never have suspected my Jack would be involved in something like this. It doesn't make me proud. Sure as there is whiskey in Ireland that this garbage has to do with Jack's death. Who's the guy they found?"

— "We don't know yet, he hasn't opened his mouth. We've got his car, we'll get the registration, by noon we'll know this guy's life's story. Soon enough he'll talk, you've seen the type before, they keep silent for a day. We'll have to be patient. But I tell you something, this guy did not kill Jack, he could have taken all the bricks after he killed the kids. He had all night and the next day to move the stuff. And you and I agree that it was two men that killed Jack, two men could have moved all the bricks inside one hour."

— "Gene, I think you should charge him just the same, that will make the real killer feel at ease. Charge him, have the drugs destroyed, let the State take the house. Who cares? Charge him, let it make the news tonight. I'm going home, I had enough."

— "Home to Orlando?"

— "No, home to Patrick's house. I need a break. I'll call you."

John was at his brother's house shortly after eight in the morning and walked into the kitchen to make himself coffee. There was nobody in the house. Carol Mackenzie called John's cellular at five pass two. "Captain Kazmierski said to call you, May I come over?"

— "You do that, we'll talk. Later I'll take you to eat out. Now listen up, this is not a date, I'm not in the mind frame for dates. I'm so ashamed Carol, Patricia was right, I did not know my son. Come over around five." John drove to Patrick's hardware store in Arlington Heights to tell him about the plants, and warned him there will be hordes of television people coming up to interview him. John had rented a car and planned to drive to a hotel near the airport to spend the night away from the television cameras.

Carol met John at the Mall, they went to a movie and spoke little and drove in two cars to a sports bar after, ordered Pub grub and drank Lagers. "What made you come to Chicago?"

— "I wanted to be in law enforcement since high school, Philadelphia was not a good choice. I'd been in Chicago for tennis tournaments and I liked it. I came straight out of Penn State and applied to the Police Academy. There was no man involved."

— "There must have been a man at some point."

— "There was; So? There is no man now, I had a boyfriend but not any longer. Nobody you know."

— "I have no one in Florida either." John wanted to talk, had so much to say but did not know how.

— "Do you want to talk about Jack's house? You have to talk to someone John, it's healthy." They were sitting on opposite sides of a table and Carol extended her hands to hold John's. His hands were ice cold. "You're cold John."

— "I know. What day is today?"

— "Wednesday. It'll be Christmas in a few weeks, we'll go somewhere together."

— "We'll see. I don't know what I want to do next. I don't feel good."

— "Come with me to my apartment, stay with me."

— "No, not now, let's go." John dropped three twenties on the table and they walked to Carol's car, the license plate read CLUFINDR. "You never told me your other handle." John put his hands on Carol's waist and pulled her toward him to kiss her, and Carol put her arms inside John's and hug him at the waist. They pressed their bodies together and kissed for a long time. "It's easy to fall in love with you, Carol, you're a special woman. This is very new to me." They kissed more. Carol went to talk but John put his hand on her lips. "Don't say anything, we'll talk soon. I need to be alone for a while, have to think. I'll be back before Sunday night. I'm in love with you Carol. Don't say anything. Get in the car, it's cold."

— "Come with me."

— "No." And he walked away and was half way to his car when he heard Carol.

— "John." He turned around. "They call me Chunky."

John spent the night in a Holiday Inn near the airport and when he could not fall asleep John found a comedy with Michael Douglass and Kathleen Turner in a pay channel. At eight was driving north on Interstate 55 on his way to Milwaukee. He had questions to ask but the picture was clearer now.

CHAPTER 7
MILWAUKEE

THE NAME OF THE firm was Terrapin, Adamson & Jones Financial Consultants. John telephoned as he passed Kenosha, Mr. Adamson had had a death in the family and was not expected back for at least one week, his personal secretary's secretary was taking messages, anything urgent will be addressed by Mr. Terrapin Junior. John was able to reach Adamson's personal secretary and explained he was Jack's father and left his cell number for Mr. Adamson to call him back. The call came as he was reaching Milwaukee.

— "I apologize for not having the courage to call you yesterday, I'm not all together. I'd like to meet with you, maybe your wife too. I'll be in Milwaukee in twenty minutes, you tell me."

— "We're actually at our country house in Lake Geneva, we drove on Sunday night with our older son, his wife and children. Thank heavens we're all here, my house and my office have been bombarded with phone calls after last night's news. We're afraid the news people will follow us here."

— "They will. If you want to be left alone, your best bet is to go to a friend's house or book a hotel in your wife's maiden name somewhere far. They won't leave you alone. Ours is the sort of news that sells newspapers. Anyway, I would like to talk to you, and your wife as well. We all need to understand the problem before we look for a solution. Is it all right if I drive up? You may give me directions once I'm closer. And think about driving somewhere else, it's been eighteen hours since this went public. By now I'm sure they have your country address and they'll come in helicopters. Think about it. Did my cell number show in yours?"

— "It did."

— "I'll keep driving, should be in Lake Geneva in a couple of hours. Call me."

Mr. Adamson's call came only fifteen minutes later. "We're taking your advice, we'll be driving to my partner's lodge in Sturgeon Bay. We're all going, in two vehicles. We'd like you to come over, we're so glad you warned us, please join us. Drive straight to Sturgeon Bay, it's north and east of Green Bay, we'll give you directions to the lodge once we're there, we're not sure ourselves how to get to it. Thanks." And he hung up before John could answer.

John stopped for dinner on the way and read the Chicago Tribune as he waited for Adamson's call. By eight o'clock no call had come so he telephoned Adamson. "We were waiting for your call, worried you may have had an accident." So far communicating with Adamson had not been clear. John wrote down the directions, many small roads and many turns. It took an hour and ten minutes to drive thirty miles. The lodge had a third of a mile private drive leading to it; it'd be hard for news people to get in, it would be trespassing, but then news people have their own rules.

A man in a Suburban SUV let John go through the gate. The drive to the lodge was paved and there were lamp posts along the way. The lodge was a three-story massive timber structure with a detached car garage that could easily house five cars. There was a sprinkle of snow on the lodge's roof. A man in a hunter's outfit took John's car to the garage. A second man, dressed in blue jeans and white turtleneck came out from the house and greeted John. "You must be Jack's father. Hi, I'm Sean, Christian's brother, pleased to meet you. Dad and Mom are waiting for you inside."

— "May I wash up before I see your parents?, It's been a long day." Sean walked John upstairs to a guest room. Fifteen minutes later John walked to where the voices were coming from, a double-height space with many sofas and a blazing fire. "Good evening to you all, I'm Jack's father, it seems that we should have met in better times, years ago." The older lady in the bulky sweater gave John a look that translated into 'It sure wasn't because of us'.

— "May we offer you something to eat?, You must be famished. A drink as well? There is food on the side table, help yourself. What do you drink? I'm Sarah, Sean's wife."

— "Scotch on ice, thanks. I had dinner not too long ago."

— "Our host is famous for his collection of single-malts, this one is Bellvenie, 18-years, we've left the little bit for you. Just kidding, Sean and I are the only ones who drink, Mom and Dad sip white wine." Sarah was very attractive, tall and slender, long straight blonde hair, light blue eyes, tanned with white around her eyes, a skier's tan, very long legs and a great figure that was enhanced by a thin turtleneck two sizes too small worn over her skin. Sarah must be very proud of her nipples. John had met a few wealthy women in Orlando but not in this league and felt out of place, the other four probably took notice. John walked to the fire and turned his back to it, not sure if to sit down or to stand up. The two couples were sitting two to a sofa. John chose a love seat away from the fire and sat at the edge, bending forward with the single-malt cupped in his hands. He decided he'd drink his glass slowly and would keep silent to see who will speak first, bet it would be Sarah and Sarah it was.

— "We were hoping you'd have some sort of explanation for what happened." Suddenly John had this weird thought that the assassin's target was Christian and that Jack was collateral damage, as they say in the military after forty children are shredded into pieces by some jerk who had not yet mastered the intricacies of his missile guidance system.

— "If you refer to my son's and your brother in law's assassinations, all I can say is that the bulk of the Chicago Police force is working intensely to capture the one who did it. If you refer to the plants in Jack's and Christian's house so far all that has happened is that somebody who has a key to the house broke in, surely to take drugs with him." John was edgy and feeling out of place.

— "Well, not drugs, it was only grass, grass is not really drugs."

— "Sarah, I did not drive ten hours to be confrontational, I came here to befriend Christian's parents. Nevertheless, in the State of Illinois marihuana is an illegal substance, a drug. Its possession is punishable by law. It is a federal crime as well. Ten ounces will get you in big trouble, there are six hundred kilos in bricks stored in the house."

— "You saw it?" It was Christian's father who asked.

— "I did. There is no mistake about it. You all know I've been a policeman for twenty-five years. To be sincere, I don't know what my reaction would be had Jack been alive.

— "It may be best if we all go to bed now, we're all tired. Let's rest and join for breakfast tomorrow, we'll talk in the morning. Mr. O'Rourke, my husband

and I loved your son, he was a fine young man, like a son to us. And we're very happy that finally we got to meet you. Sarah, you and Sean go along, the three of us will follow." Mrs. Adamson showed her good sense. "We all had a hard day, especially you Mr. O'Rourke; May I call you John? No alarm clocks for us, let us sleep as much as our bodies need, no schedule, we get up when we get up. You never remarried John, Did you?" John shook his head once. "We'll drink coffee in the den, we'll have a nice brunch. All right with you?" John had the distinct impression that Mrs. Adamson wasn't thrilled with Sarah.

John fell asleep as he put his head down and woke up at ten, his best sleep since he had left Orlando. The Adamsons were waiting for him in the den next to the kitchen; there were several plates with breads, cheeses, fruits and other foods on a side board, sliced bread next to a toaster and a fondue pot with boiling cheese. For no reason at all, John remembered his mother saying that if he did not eat all his food the children of China would go hungry and remembered too that he never understood the rational; surely Mom knew better. He served himself coffee and buttered a slice of toasted rye; John sat to the left of Mrs. Adamson, facing her husband. John figured the Adamsons to be about ten years older than him, maybe more. He bit into the toast and realized he had drunk all his coffee and went for more.

— "It is best if it is only the three of us." John bit the toast again, obviously the Adamsons had eaten their brunch earlier. "I prefer to go to the point and be candid but I don't want the two of you to find me rude." The look in their faces told John to move forward. "We have to be sincere with each other. I would like to know if you suspected the drug business." John selected 'suspected' as being harmless. "Please tell me."

— "Christian had done it before, when he was twenty or maybe a teenager, you know Christian was six years older than Jack." John went to the side board for more coffee, no toast this time. Mrs. Adamson waited for John to come back before continuing. "My sister had cancer and Christian grew marihuana in pots in the balcony at home in Milwaukee and made cigarettes for Mary Ellen, it helped her along with the pain; of course, it came a time when she was given morphine, but Mary Ellen smoked Christian's cigarettes for a good three years. Because of the cold Christian brought the pots inside. In the spring and summer he grew plants in the old house in Lake Geneva, lots of plants."

— "Was Christian ever in trouble with the law?"

55

— "No, he was not. Dad and I never looked at Christian's plants as a criminal act, I guess we may have been wrong. We figured they were for sick people."

— "It's a criminal offense, and if you sell the punishment is severe." John paused. "I've made up my mind I'm going to put the plants aside, I'm only keen on helping the police find and convict the one who killed our sons. I don't see a connection between the plants and the killings." The lady started to cry. "I'm sorry Mrs. Adamson, I don't mean to be callous, it's just the way I speak, I'm truly sorry." John waited.

It was Mr. Adamson who spoke. "Today's Tribune says the man they captured in the house may be the one who killed the children. We saw his photograph in the paper, we've met him at Christian's house, at a dinner party. He's a lawyer."

John was surprised. "More will be learned as my colleagues talk to him. Keep in mind that so far this man is only a suspect, he may very well be just a thief, not necessary the murderer. In my profession one does not jump to conclusions, one collects data and puts it together, crimes are solved with hundreds of short steps, not a big leap. Let me go to the point. I hardly knew my son, I'm ashamed to tell, but that's the case, can't change that now. I don't know his friends, Christian I met only twice, never had much of a conversation with him. The question is: Do you know anybody that may have a reason for killing your son, not my son, your son? That's what will help, anybody, any reason. And the same in relation to Jack. My colleagues are searching for a motive." Both Adamsons shook their heads. John had driven three hundred miles for three cups of coffee and two slices of toast.

— "One last thought, if Jack and Christian have been growing marihuana in the same scale since they moved into their house a year and a half ago I figured they made several million dollars. Where is the money? Who buys it? Answers may lead us to the killer. Anyway, I wish our children were alive and I had met you under better circumstances. I'll be leaving soon, I need to be in Chicago tonight."

— "You are from Chicago, Aren't you?" Mrs. Adamson asked. "So am I, born and raised, I moved to Milwaukee after I married Chris. I miss Chicago. I lived in the City, went to Lincoln High, my maiden name is DiRenzo." Mrs. Adamson was giving John a message, and her husband squeezed her arm. "Honey, you may want to go upstairs and change so we may go later for your walk."

— "I'm not up to it Chris, Why don't you take John with you instead and talk to him, go ahead and talk to him?" Mrs. Adamson emphasized 'talk' and made it very obvious.

— "Honey, John has to be in Chicago tonight and it's a long ride, I'll show John to his car. We'll take our walk later. You rest until then, I'll stay outdoors." And walked towards John, forcing this to walk towards the door.

— "I meant to ask both of you something and I forgot. Has any of you seen Stephen Vesic lately?" John planted himself solidly on his feet and Mr. Adamson backed down.

— "I don't believe we know anybody of that name, Do we, Honey?, From Milwaukee?, Chicago? What line of business is he in?" Mr. Adamson had lost his smile.

— "Muskegon, Michigan. Vesic is in the export business, car parts. Maybe at the party at Christian? See if you can remember. "Will you ask Sean? Where is he? I'd like to say good bye."

— "Sean and Sarah went out with one of the men, hunting I guess. They were up early." Mrs. Adamson had a smirk on her face. "Sarah was a bit of an embarrassment last night, it's the drink." Mrs. Adamson did not approve of thin tight turtlenecks with no underwear.

— "Pleasure meeting you Ma'am." Mr. Adamson's body language was asking John to leave. "Let me go fetch my bag. I'll be a minute." Mr. Adamson was standing in the porte-cochere next to John's Chrysler.

— "Nice car."

— "It's a rental. In Orlando I drive a red Carrera." John came very close to Mr. Adamson. "Listen Adamson, we can do this friendly or unfriendly. You talk to me now like your wife told you to do or I'll see you get a subpoena on Monday and I'll drag you all the way to Chicago, please don't tell me how big a lawyer you have, I guarantee you'll be in an interrogation room inside a week, and Mrs. Adamson, and young Sean and sweet Sarah too. On drug charges. For starters, Who handles the money? Is it you or Sean? Don't lie to me, I have Jack's spreadsheet from his computer, I have Jack's e-mails and I have Christian's too. It's easy to follow the money trail, you'll have to explain five million in cash. The IRS's limit is what? Ten thousand? Your partner with the big lodge won't be happy either. Better talk to me now, if you don't I'll be on my cellular the moment I get in my car. And for whatever is worth to you, several people know I'm here. Second, I want Jack's half, two-and-a-

57

half-million, and I want it now. How soon can you transfer? And don't tell me how complicated it is, you're the financier."

— "My field is tax accounting, Sean is an investments consultant. Jack's and Christian's money is in securities in several accounts with European banks and it's not even close to that sum. Including profits from the investments is just under three million, half of it is Jack's. We need at least two months not to be at risk. Neither Sean nor I ever intended to withhold Jack's share." Sure, and I'll love you in the morning Hon.

— "We'll settle on a million-five, half in thirty days, half at the end of January, how you do it is your problem, I don't care to know. Don't disappoint me, Adamson, half thirty-one December, half thirty-one January. I'll let you know where to transfer. Tell me about Vesic, When did you see him last?"

— "Never heard the name." Drops of perspiration were coming down the man's temples; it was under thirty degrees in the porte-cochere. "You'll have Jack's share as you asked. Now please leave."

John decided he'd figure out what to do with Jack's money later. Now he was to concentrate on the murders, Jack's murder, he had a different vision now than two days earlier. It was already afternoon and he was still north of Green Bay. The cellular was not working, he'd have to wait until he reached the city. By the time he had a signal it was past three, he rang Monty DeSimone's office.

— "Sorry Mr. O'Rourke, Mr DeSimone took Friday off. Care to go to voice-mail?"

— "No, May I have his cellular?"

— "I'm so-o-o sorry, I'm not allowed. I could lose my job."

— "I'll leave a message with Mrs. Peterson, it has to do with certain books Jack left in his office anyway."

Mrs. Peterson had Monty's number. "Monty, it's John O'Rourke, I need to talk to you, in person, it has to do with something Jack said to me on the phone about a client of yours. It may be relevant to your client." That much should suffice.

— "I'm not in my office, off today, I'm working on my boat, I'll be here tomorrow and Sunday all day, I'm staying in the boat. Why don't you come over to the Club tomorrow late morning, we'll have lunch at the bar, Does it work for you?" It did suffice.

John spent the night at a Marriott in Kenosha, got up early and was at the Yacht Club's gate at eleven. Monty had announced a guest at the gate without leaving a name and the guard showed John where to park. This soon realized he was dressed very wrong, but there was not much he could do. Monty had said to go to the bar; Monty was waiting there. "Are you ready for lunch or rather have a drink and go check the boats for a while, it's a little early for me." John ordered a beer and they walked outside. "I'll take you see my boat first, the love of my life. I have this guilt I'm betraying my love for a newer boat. But that's life, isn't it."

The motor boats and the small sail boats where arranged by size along piers and the large sail boats were anchored scattered over the basin. Monty's sailboat was a forty footer painted bright lime green with white sails, to John it looked brand new. "What's wrong with it? It looks new to me."

— "Nothing is wrong, it's a great boat but it's a cruising boat not a racer. I'll be working just to pay for the new boat, better get used to sleeping here, may have to give up the apartment. Jack and Christian sailed with me many times, not in races, just cruising. Jack liked to call other boats on the radio, I have a satellite radio, Jack had fun with it."

— "You said you race. Do you race this boat?"

— "I do, now and then, other people's boats too. You realize that a six-hour race may be lost, or won, by a fraction of a minute; one bad tack will lose it for you." They had finished their beers. "Want to see something spectacular? Let's go see the yachts, we've got the best in the lake. Remember the company Jack worked on, that one is theirs, hundred and fifty footer, watch the lines, carries enough fuel to sail from Boston to Cannes, better instruments than the U.S. Navy, the Yacht Club's pride, our 'Julia', What do you say?"

— "I say I could get used to living on that boat if I could afford the fuel. What size crew?"

— "It takes an experienced captain and two good hands, these things don't have brakes. The captain makes more than a junior accountant, weekend guests tip him in the hundreds, and the hands make half the captain's wage. Plus a cook unless one of the hands cooks. Tanks for four thousand gallons of diesel, two engines, six state rooms, accommodates twelve guests overnight

59

comfortably. If they gave that yacht to you and me, we could not afford the crew, the fuel and the insurance. It takes mucho, mucho money."

— "You've been on it then."

— "Not yet."

— "And a company owns it?"

— "Yes, and since it's used for business entertainment is a tax deduction. How do you like them apples? Isn't capitalism wonderful?"

— "What does the company make that pays for the boat?"

— "Bombs."

— "Bombs?"

— "Bombs, for Uncle Sam, three products, one client, production contracted for as long as six years, it's like printing money. Family owned company, the company Jack did the audit for, second generation. The founder has been dead for some time, I never met the old man. They are very proud of him, very clever man, an inventor. Russian, was in the revolution with Trotsky, Do you know Russian history? After Lenin died Stalin deported Trotsky to Turkey, I believe nineteen-twenty-nine. Trotsky had to leave in a hurry and ended in Mexico where he got killed in nineteen-forty by his gardener, who stuck an axe in Trotsky's skull; Stalin was not the kind of guy who forgot or forgave. So after Trotsky left Russia the old man, who was in his early thirties then and had been making bombs since he was twelve, had to leave in a hurry too so he went next door to Germany and got a job. Where? In a bombs factory, Where else? By the time the Nazi's were in control the old man had devised some gadgets and some manufacturing process so he turned into a big wheel in a munitions plant; the guy went from Communist to Nazi inside five years, so much for his convictions. At the end of the war the old man was snatched by the U.S.Army Intelligence people, was taken to North Carolina, all sins forgotten, and was given a job to design I guess bombs. In the fifties the old man moved to Illinois to chase the American dream and started a small plant, had maybe ten or twenty people, most likely all resettled Nazi's, sold all his production to Uncle Sam. One customer, sure pay, no hassles, better than you and me. Let's walk back to bar, we'll eat lunch. Am I boring you?"

— "No, it's fascinating."

— "Vietnam happens, the firm grows to over two hundred people, they built

acility west of Chicago, state of the art with very tight security which
;ely the way Uncle Sam likes it, and our buddy the former communist
metimes Nazi starts making money like there is no tomorrow. The
.an's son is no inventor but he's a brilliant tinkerer. So the company
the patents of several good products and the son changes them from
l to great, now they have twice as many people and make three times as
:h money. Ordinance becomes very complicated, smart bombs guided by
:tronics, these guys make the best. Their explosive packs three times the
ng of anything else. You want to kill a goat from two hundred miles, never
ar, they'll figure it out how. Money, money, money. Competition got stiff
n the nineties, never affected them, they kept making a ton of money. The
old communist died in his late eighties, the son runs the company. Born in
Germany in the thirties, before the war, he's got to be around seventy-five."

— "You know the man?"

— "From the club. We don't do their books, they've consulted with us from
time to time, they use in-house help, not a good policy, anyway I'm good
friends with their Comptroller, good guy, I'm working hard to get their
business. So far they gave us the limited review, the one Jack worked on, and
I'm trying to land the going public offering. We'll see. I was invited to their
Christmas party next week, Jack was too. A big event. There'll be generals,
the Governor, the Mayor, it's a more difficult ticket than the Superbowl. Last
Christmas they brought Willy Nelson. I have Jack's ticket, Would you like
to attend?"

— "May I take a date?"

— "The detective you brought along?"

— "How can you tell?" Monty laughed all the way to the bar.

— "I'll see what I can do. It may be best if I don't ask for another ticket, I
don't have that much clout and they could decide that they invited Jack, not
you. Do you want to risk it? No way to crash this place, the party is at the
factory's offices and they don't let anybody in without the ticket. There'll be
security guards up the gazzoo. Actually you have to go through security, worse
than airports, cars stay outside. I didn't get the invitation from the company,
Julia invited me."

— "Julia the yacht?"

— "Jack got his sense of humor from you. Listen, they have a fixed menu,

61

they'll serve when it's our turn, you'll get a fresh drink when they see that yours is near empty until you say stop." Two glasses of Pilsner arrived unannounced. "Julia is Mr. Taylor's daughter."

— "Hold on, you said they are Russian and lived in Germany. Where does the name Taylor come from?"

— "I don't know the old man's Russian name, but I heard that in Germany the old man changed it to Schneider, it means tailor. That's my guess; listen, I'm an accountant not a detective."

— "Jack said to me once that an accountant is a detective for figures."

— "True. An audit is an investigation." Monty sipped his beer. "Anyways, Julia is not in the bombs factory, I told you Julia owns a catering company, she services this club, our cafeteria and runs the best weddings in Chicago. Very successful company, very smart woman, pretty too, younger than us. You'll meet her at the party, Julia is nice."

— "And single?"

— "As far as I know. There is a bad joke that circulates in the club. I shouldn't laugh, they probably have half a dozen jokes about me."

— "Does that bother you?"

— "Of course it does. No matter how much I excel at everything I'm still the fag. I can win fifty races, I'm still the fag. It goes with the territory and anybody that says you get used to it is not truthful. Jack did not talk much to you, Right?"

— "No, it's my fault."

— "Let it go. Can't do much now, my father never said a word to me, he's dead now." Lunch started with New England chowder. "You said you have something to tell me."

— "And I do. The last time Jack telephoned me he talked about what he was doing and said to me and I quote 'Somebody is robbing these people blind', exactly that, word by word, 'Somebody is robbing these people blind'. At the time I didn't give it any thought but now I think it may be related to what happened to Jack. What do you think?"

— "Well, it's really not news to me. Jack told me too, and to Mr. Taylor and to Ben Piesecki their Comptroller at the meeting in Jack's office. Mr.

Taylor told me as he was leaving the meeting, he was very upset. He said Jack had done a great job although he was not happy with what Jack found out. Jack found discrepancies in the records that Piesecki had overlooked. Apparently it happened during the last five years and they are not optimistic about retrieving their moneys but they'll try." The second course was trout Meuniere, DeSimone ordered a White Zinfandel to go with it.

— "What about the Vesic character? Did you find him? Tell me about the key."

— "Vesic owns an import-export company in Michigan. We're still searching for him, sooner or later he'll pop up, it's a matter of time. Then we'll talk to him."

CHAPTER 8
GIANNI

ON SUNDAY NIGHT, CAROL and John drove to dinner in Carol's Mazda two-seater with the CLUFINDR license plate and the valet asked Carol if she was a journalist. "Just make sure it won't get scratched and I'll tip you two nickels."

— "You found a nice place for our second date. Been here before?"

— "No."

— "Good, let's order wine. How about a Chianti? I'm going to eat pasta, I dieted since you left and I deserve it. So what did you do since last Thursday?"

— "I drove to Wisconsin and met Christian's parents and older brother, very nice people, I plan to stay in touch with them."

By the time they finished dessert Carol had learned everything she wanted to know about John. "So you said before you have a new point of view about Vesic."

— "I may have it all wrong, the message I mean. It may be that Vesic does not have a key, it may be that Vesic is the key."

— "And the figures?"

— "I don't know for sure but I suspect is the amount of money somebody took from the company Jack audited, over twelve million dollars."

— "The key to what?"

— "I suppose to the stolen money. We'll ask Vesic, sooner or later he'll show up somewhere."

— "And you're sure that Vesic is connected to the murders?"

— "I'm not, but so far Vesic is our one lead, he may have stolen the money, he may be in cahoots with those who stole the money, and these may have wanted to silence Jack before he went too far with his reports. We'll have to talk to Vesic to find out."

Carol and John spent twenty minutes talking in the car at John's hotel's parking lot before Carol drove away and John entered the lobby. The blonde with the very short hair and platform shoes stood up as soon as John retrieved his key and followed him to the elevator, chatting on her cellular non stop. Pint-size and pretty, the blonde favored cheap perfume and made up in quantity what it lacked in quality. "Push ten for me please." John did, his floor was nine, he waited for the blonde to offer her friendship but she did not.

— "You a reporter?"

— "No, I'm an artist." The blond was leaning on the rear wall and John had to turn around to talk to her. The door opened and John stepped out, the blonde kept chatting. The three men were waiting in front of the elevator, two were professional wrestler size. The three got very close to John. "You have nothing to fear. Our boss wants a word with you. We work for Mr. DiRenzo." John figured if they wanted to kill him they could have done it as soon as he stepped out of the elevator. "Walk with us, Mr. DiRenzo is waiting for you." The two wrestlers walked behind John and the one who knew how to speak lead the way. "Mr. DiRenzo said you may keep your piece, we'll be outside, step in." The room was twice the size as John's and had a seating area with a sofa and two stuffed chairs in front of a television set more than twice the size the one in John's room. Gianni DiRenzo was watching a hockey game, looked like the Penguins and the Flyers; on the coffee table there were several plastic cups, an ice bucket with no ice and a dozen miniature liquor bottles, several empty, and opened bags of peanuts and crackers.

— "The shit they put in the minibar here is the worse I've seen, you ought to be able to afford a better joint, Johnny, you used to be a class act. Excuse me I don't get up, they gave me a new pair of hips and I'm learning to walk again. So, how've you been Johnny? Orlando, isn't it? Yeah, you look good Johnny, you have a tan. Help yourself to a drink." DiRenzo looked old and soft, he had gained weight and his big frame was slumped, and much of his hair had turned white. He was wearing a brown sports jacket over an unbuttoned yellow shirt, not the sharp dresser he used to be. John figured DiRenzo to be approaching seventy.

— "You don't look bad yourself. What's with the secret meeting?" Johnny was not sure if to call him Mr. DiRenzo or Gianni.

— "You treated yourself better when you were in my payroll Johnny, your room isn't even as nice as this one and this is shitty. Short of funds, Johnny? No wonder your girlfriend didn't come up and went home." John did not appreciate Gianni's comment but did not answer. "I thought you detectives were not allowed to, How do I say this? Fraternize. Are you fraternizing that young woman Johnny? She real cute. "

— "Payroll?" John took his jacket off and laid it on the bed, he pulled his holster with the semi-automatic and laid it on top of the jacket, and threw a pillow on top.

— "Yeah, payroll. Didn't you use to get a slice of my envelope? Please don't tell me that your buddies never cut you in. Listen, babe, my father paid to do business, I pay to do business and if I had a son he'd pay to do business. You were in my payroll Johnny and that's all right, so long as you remember. This is Chicago, everybody makes a living."

— "So what is you want to tell me?"

— "I ain't telling you, you're telling me. You've been harassing my sister Johnny, can't do that. Fuck is with you? You lost your manners? My sister called me and said you're threatening her. Something about a subpoena. Are you out of your fucking mind?"

— "Bullshit, Gianni. Adamson called you, not your sister. Your sister clued me in, she wanted to help me. It's her fuck husband who called you. You tell me." John sat down and emptied a miniature bottle of Jack Daniels in his cup. Have any ice? Never mind." He took a sip. "I want Jack's money and Adamson was chiseling me, I wanted to shake him up. Didn't register Mrs. Adamson was your sister."

— "They both called me. Adamson is shitting in his pants and my sister likes you. So you were kidding then?" DiRenzo emptied a little bottle of V.O. into his half-full glass and dripped some on the table. "Good, you don't want to find yourself swimming half way to Michigan with your feet stuck in a cement bucket. So tell me you didn't talk to your buddies." DiRenzo took a long sip and kept the plastic cup touching his lips. "Tell me."

— "I didn't. But I want Jack's money. I figured they made five mil, I want Jack's half. I saw the place and I know how long they've been selling. I can do the math."

— "You know shit, you think you know, you don't."

— "So you bankrolled them?" John sipped his whiskey.

— "No I didn't. I'm into gaming, I don't do no grass. I'm in the casinos now, big time, I'm with the Indians in Missouri, doing good, could make you head of security in our new place, we'll be opening in eight months if we can get all the fucking permits. There is a third guy, the kid your buddies pinched in Christian's house, Sunny Alvarez. They cut the profit into three."

— "How would you know?"

— "Christian was like a son to me, he spent more weekends with me than with his father. When he was a teenager Chris came to Chicago on weekends and stayed in my house.

— "And who's Sunny?"

— "Sunny and Christian are friends since their college days. They were growing and selling grass long before Christian met your son. I knew Jack, great kid. The whole thing is a fucking shame. Tell me something, Are you looking for the killer on your own? Or with your pals?"

— "On my own. I help them and they help me, but I'm on my own."

— "And if you find him, What?"

— "I have to see about that."

— "Bullshit Johnny. I remember the fuck that raped and strangled the two little sisters, they put you and your partner after that guy, yous guys found him, yous went fishing to Florida and the guy was never seen again. What was his name? Nostradamus or something? It's been a long time and everybody forgot about the guy but I remember, you can tell me now."

— "I don't even know what you're talking about. Let's stay with Sunny." John had to decide if the Kopernik's question was DiRenzo's threat or if he was only curious.

— "Christian and your son grew the plants, did all the labor, packaged the bricks. Sunny sold the product. They never crossed lines. Their biggest challenge was getting rid of the waste, you end with a lot of shit after you harvest. They couldn't burn it, they had to bag it and truck it far away. Risky, but the kids managed it. They would rent a van and drive west to Iowa, sometimes down to Missouri. That part worried me sick. I offered to have my people get rid of the waste, they never took me up, I guess they felt safer if no one else was involved."

— "How often did you see Christian? And my Jack?"

— "All the time. We ate together at my restaurant every couple of weeks, I took the kids to the Cubs's games, I have a box behind first base. The kids trained in one of my gyms, I have an office there. I'm telling you, Christian was like my own son."

— "And Sunny sold to whom?"

— "At the beginning to groups that distribute to sick people, they gave some away too. But last year they doubled the production so I got them an outlet. People I know."

— "Who?"

— "Who? You're a cop, I ain't gonna tell you. You out of your fucking mind?"

— "The buyer may be the one who killed them."

— "No fucking way. They was making good money out of the kids, Why would they kill them? Everybody knows Christian is my kid, you know people don't fuck with me. Listen up, everybody I know, everybody who knows everybody I know and everybody who knows them are looking for the fuck who killed our kids. I put a hundred grand contract on the fuck. I don't want him dead, I want him delivered to me, You understand? Or you want me to paint you a picture?"

— "This Sunny is a lawyer, right?"

— "Sunny is all right, I've known him for years, he's a kid from Cicero, he bought his father a restaurant, the guy can't cook shit and he's the chef, they even had him in the television, he's a celebrity now. Sunny came to see me at the hospital the day the kids were killed, that's why he can't talk, can't get me mixed with the plants. He was with me till past seven. Sunny's a tough kid, he kept his mouth shut. He'll be all right." DiRenzo stuck his right hand in the ice bucket and all he found was cold water. "You mind going to the door and ask Pauly to get us some ice, we're gonna be here for a while, we've got a lot of talking to do." John walked to the door and waited for the bucket to come back. The two wrestlers stood in front of him, each looked wider than the door. "Sunny's a lawyer and nobody in his firm would represent him, imagine that. I sent him a lawyer, not mine but a big deal lawyer, he'll work something out, Sunny ain't doing time. What did you tell Adamson?"

— "I told Adamson I want Jack's money. I figured two-and-a-half mil give or take and Adamson started whinnying that there isn't that much. Jack left notes with the amount. Actually your sister's son handled the money."

— "Stepson."

— "Meaning?"

— "Adamson was married before and had a son and a daughter, his wife died. The daughter lives in the west coast. The son Sean is a bit of an asshole, my sister don't like him much. Sean always kept Christian at a distance, away from his friends, Country Club shit if you ask me." DiRenzo put too much ice in his cup and was trying to take some out. "Chris first grew grass for my sister Mary Ellen that had cancer and when he went to college he and Sunny had plants all around Milwaukee, in empty lots, roadsides. They let the plants grow wild and pulled them out when they were ready. Soon they had a business, the kids were smart. Very careful too, never got in trouble."

— "My son too?"

— "No, Christian did not meet Jack until five, six years ago. I'm talking fifteen years here, I think they grew plants all through college, they always had money, smart kids."

— "So Jack started when?"

— "Christian and Jack bought the house and they remodeled, and they were always short of money because they took a big mortgage. So they closed half the basement, put a generator and the lights and it was like printing money. Them two and Sonny, I've been at their house, I've seen it. Their biggest problem was to get rid of the plants once they pulled them out, lots of waste."

— "And you never distributed for them?"

— "I told you I'm into gaming, I don't need problems, I have it easy. I helped

69

them out, I gave Christian a couple of names here and in Detroit so they could move it."

— "So they made a lot of cash and they gave the cash to Adamson, Right?"

— "Yeah, and Adamson got his older son Sean involved. You know Adamson's son was in Chicago with his wife the night the kids were killed, they left the children with my sister in Milwaukee. Adamson's son put the kid's money in Europe."

— "And you think that was smart?"

— "No I don't. I could have put their money in the casino or in Vegas."

— "And you know how much they had?"

— "I do, Christian told me three months ago the pie was getting close to five million dollars, so divide that by three and your son's got around a million-five. You'll get Jack's share. Listen, my sister liked Jack a great deal and she doesn't want Adamson's son to stiff you. My sister doesn't like the son-of-a-bitch much. She's the one that told me about your trip there." There were no more V.O. bottles so DiRenzo switched to Cutty. "If you want my advice, settle for one-point-five and have them hand you the money in cash in Mexico or Canada. Don't take no paper. I can place it for you in Vegas if you want, you'll clear fifteen percent per year, cash, can't beat that. You let me know. Now listen."

— "I've been listening for over two hours."

— "Right, so listen some more. You forget about this subpoena shit and call Adamson and tell him. And tell him you want your money now. You don't need to scare them, they're already shitting bricks, father and son. I never understood why my sister married that guy, she should have married somebody from the neighborhood, a good Italian guy."

— "Somebody like you?"

— "You've got it. Is there anything else you may want to tell me? Don't hide from me Johnny." DiRenzo had to use both hands to push himself out of the chair and stand up, and each step to the bathroom was an effort. He came back after the Penguins had scored two goals. "I can hardly walk, I'm still doing my therapy. I only came out to make sure you're not doing something stupid. You was always smart Johnny, better stay that way. Now, I'm gonna ask you again. Is there anything else you may want to tell me?" DiRenzo moved back in the chair to prop his lower back.

— "I guess there is. Jack was doing some kind of an audit for his company and found out somebody had stolen over twelve million dollars, and told the owners the same day he was killed. I'm following that angle, if I can find the one who stole the twelve mil I may have the killer. Also, Jack left a paper folded in a book with a name, Stephen Vesic. I met this character in a club in Old Town and he gave me the slip. I'm looking for him."

— "Good, I'm glad you told me. I know all about it. Go tell Pauly to get us a few more of these bottles. Tell him to go to your room. And some of this shit to eat." John used the bathroom before he sat down.

— "And how do you know that?"

— "I still send an envelope every two weeks. Your buddies keep me posted. I put the word out about Vesic and got something back the next morning. This Vesic plays in one of my games in Cicero, he's good, prefers straight poker but will play any kind, the guy wins, makes good money and a bunch of suckers want to play him. You know we give a shit who wins, we take our five percent from each pot, no matter to us."

— "You know where to find Vesic?"

— "Not yet, but I'll soon find out where this Vesic lives, I've got plenty of people looking. Vesic talked a lot at the table and my guys talked to our dealers and to several regulars that played Vesic. You know, guys he had a couple of beers with or ate dinner with. So this is the deal, I'm gonna point Vesic to you and you're gonna tell me everything Vesic says, and I mean everything. What I care for is what you find out, I get what your buddies find out the morning after. I have my chips on you Johnny, you're good at your shit. A capito?"

— "I got you. We have a deal. You'll know everything I know."

— "Don't disappoint me Johnny, you know how this stuff works. I've got your word now." Pauly came in with the ice bucket and carried miniature bottles and snacks in a pillow case that he emptied on top of the bed. "Thank you Pauly, see that you and your guys get something to eat."

Both took a moment to fill new plastic cups with ice and scotch whiskey. "I found out about Vesic with the help of Jack's secretary, Vesic's got an office near the port, there is nothing there, and I mean nothing, not even a telephone. Vesic ships car parts out of Muskegon. He was arrested there twice, gambling. You may want to follow that lead. Vesic plays chess so I'm looking for him in chess clubs in Chicago. I believe I did not leave anything out."

— "Good, I already know all that shit. Vesic is Serbian, has a Serbian passport, is fifty-one or fifty-two, single, he's been living in Chicago for four, five, six years, maybe longer than that. Vesic travels to Europe, is a big spender, likes the ladies and the ladies like him. He goes to soccer games regularly, has played poker in my Cicero place for better than one year and is a winner, and talks big about being a chess player. Vesic lives in Old Town, rents an apartment, we'll find out exactly where soon. Drives a Toyota. Does not drink when he plays but drinks plenty afterwards, he drinks plum brandy, nothing else, buys only the best, hundred bucks a pop, buys it in two liquor stores in Old City, we're watching both of them, Vesic can't take a piss in Chicago without me finding out an hour later. My guys talked to the kid in the chess place, the one you scared to death, the kid's looking for Vesic for us too, he ain't gonna tell you, he'll tell us so you leave the poor fart alone." They drank in silence. "Now the bad part, nobody has seen Vesic since he ditched you, he has not shown up for poker either."

— "We'll have to be patient, Vesic will show up sooner or later. After I get some sleep I'm driving to Muskegon to see if I can find him there."

— "You want one of my boys to help you out?" The question was superfluous since one of Pauley's men had already installed a transmitter under John's car; DiRenzo would have a car with a directional receiver tailing John.

— "Nah, I work alone, but thanks for the offer."

— "You don't think Vesic is the one who killed the kids. Do you?"

— "He may be or he may lead us to the one who did it. We'll see."

CHAPTER 9
MUSKEGON, MICHIGAN

MONDAY STARTED WRONG, BY the time John got up it was half past noon, too many miniature bottles. John did not finish lunch until two, and by the time he got in the car it was three. The traffic going east was heavy and it was four-thirty when he left Interstate 90 east of Gary, Indiana, to go north on Interstate 196, finally made Muskegon at a quarter past seven. John checked in at a Holiday Inn on the highway and ate dinner at the steak house next door. All the time Lefty Gualdieri and his brother Enrico were one to two miles behind John, well out of sight and within the four mile radius their receiver allows. They checked in at the Ramada Inn nearby and took with them a gadget that would beep as soon as John's car moved. In other circumstances Enrico would have staid up all night in the SUV but Mr. DiRenzo had said that Johnny was going to the port in Muskegon so they could always pick the signal later.

On Tuesday morning John arrived at the port early, flashed his detective's badge several times and by nine he knew where to go. "I need you to please help me out, I don't know my way around here and the boss sent me to find out about somebody from Chicago who ships car parts to France. The company name is Buckingham Import-Export Company, out of Chicago. I have a name too, Vesic, Stephen Vesic. This man is what we call a person of interest, didn't do any wrong but the boss wants to interview him. You realize this is police business, please do not discuss with anybody, specially this Vesic guy, telling your boss is all right but if don't tell him is better yet." The lady was nice and helpful, she gave John a mug of good coffee and a chocolate-glazed donut and spent a long time first at a computer screen and then at two file cabinets, until she came up with one thin folder.

— "My boss is a she and I've got to tell her, but if she knows this is police business she'll keep it to herself. We get visits from agencies all the time, more about containers getting in than going out. Here is what we have on Buckingham, one folder, you may go over the pages but can't take anything away. Please stay where you are, if you need more coffee just holler, if you have to go to the bathroom, go out the door you came in and make two lefts, but let me have the folder until you come back. You got all that?" The lady left a yellow pad for John to take notes and gave him two black pens.

— "Kate, you're great help, thanks." The folder contained only receipts for fees paid to the Port of Muskegon, no bills of lading. All the shipments had been consigned by Buckingham Import-Export Company of Chicago, Illinois, to Interstate Consolidators of Muskegon, Michigan. There were eleven shipments in all, the oldest going back five years. Five deliveries made in July and five made in December, all late in the month. The only odd shipment was made four years ago in mid-March. Always one container, except for last December that shows two containers. All receipts listed 'Car Parts, New, Made in USA'.

Interstate Consolidators's offices were located at the front of a gigantic warehouse. John was told the manager would not be available for at least an hour and used his time to walk around and see the operation. There were containers everywhere, arranged in parallel lines and piled three high, and a legion of four-lift trucks collecting boxes and carrying them into open containers, where two or three hands helped stacking them. Most of the boxes came from the warehouse, wood boxes and cardboard boxes, all on wooden pallets. Other boxes came directly from delivery trucks parked in front of the warehouse. At the door of each container there was a man with a clipboard who checked what went in and noted it on some document in the clipboard. Everybody wore a hard hat.

The manager did not show up until after lunch. "What do you need to know we could not have taken care of over the telephone?" Don Aiello was a busy man and seemed to be in a hurry. "I telephoned Captain Kazmierski in your department and he said you're legit. We get a lot of snoops here so I had to check you out. The Captain said for you to call him when you're finished. So, What can I do for you?"

— "Three things. I need to confirm that your firm handled eleven shipments for Buckingham Import-Export Company during the last five years, I need to know if there were other shipments made by Buckingham, and I need to know if Buckingham has an agent other than Stephen Vesic. Also, I need their local address and I'd like to know any details about their next shipment. All of this will be kept in strict confidence and my boss would prefer if you don't give Vesic a wind of it."

— "Anything to do with terrorists?"

— "No, we believe that somebody in Chicago is selling Vesic stolen goods, we're after them, not Vesic."

— "The names, dates, anything else you want about past shipments is in the computer, you may look at it but I can't print anything out without a court order, you know that. This is a small client, they only ship twice a year, and only one container, lately two. They ship to Marseille, France, and I'll be able to tell you to whom they consign there, it's in the bill of lading. We already have freight here for their next shipment, it arrived by truck from Detroit, the day before yesterday. We're expecting more to come, so far we have a container half empty and they ordered two containers. You know Buckingham ships car parts, they come from several states, we consolidate and ship by truck to the Port of Philadelphia."

— "Not by ship?"

— "No, it's always been by truck, and always to the Port of Philadelphia. No variations."

— "When do you expect the current shipment will be completed."

— "Well, when they complete the shipment to us. We load the containers as we get the freight, and as soon as they advise us that all is in we seal the containers, load two trucks the next day and they're on their way. Our instructions are that the last delivery to us will be mid to late-December and to seal and ship after that. I expect to be done with Buckingham before December twenty."

— "Payment?"

— "Everything is prepaid here, no cash per se but cash funds, wire transfers, cashier checks, that sort of thing. Only a handful of big clients have running accounts and even with these clients it is strictly twenty-one days. Buckingham prepays with cashier checks drawn in Muskegon. We already have their funds for two containers, there will be an adjustment based on the weight, but most likely it'll be a credit to Buckingham, that's been the case so far."

— "Do you have a local address for Buckingham Import-Export Company, I mean in Muskegon, I have their place in Chicago."

— "I sure do, I'll write it down for you."

Buckingham Import-Export Company Muskegon address turned out to be a gun shop in a rundown part of town. John noticed two surveillance cameras on opposite corners of the large showroom. The wall behind the counter had a selection of semi-automatic rifles and shotguns lined up, the display counters had no fewer than two hundred hand weapons. The rest of the shop had displays of hunting gear and boots. "Hi, I'm looking for Stephen Vesic."

— "Vesic, What do you want with Vesic? Who's Vesic?"

— "Gee, at the port they gave me this address for the Buckingham Import-Export Company of Chicago and they told me Vesic is the man. I represent manufacturers of car parts in California and Oregon that want to do business with you people. I flew all the way from Portland to see Vesic."

— "Right, right. Vesic was here two weeks ago, he won't be back until June. Vesic only comes when he has to, he comes here, leaves, that's all."

— "Sure, he brings the envelop from the bank and you take it to Consolidated, Right?"

— "Yeah right. So what do you want? You a hunter?"

— "Indeed I am. And you have a heck of a selection here. What are the AK's for? Deer?"

— "No, is for collectors. You're not one of this anti-gun freaks, are you?"

— "Hell, no. I'm an NRA member, proud of it. I prize my right to be armed. How can I get ahold of Vesic?"

— "Leave your name and phone number, or leave a card, I'll give it to him when he comes in June."

— "You don't have a way to reach him?"

— "Sure I do. I have Vesic's office in Chicago, I'll give it to you."

— "I have that, but Vesic is never there. I wish you could help me more, it's good for Vesic to learn about the people I sell for, we can do business together."

— "As I said, leave your name." John left his cell number and his telephone number in Orlando.

The man followed John to the entrance door and watched John get in his car and leave, locked the entrance door and placed the steel bar across, and walked to his office to print John's picture from the surveillance cameras. He had to print a dozen until he got two clear ones. He faxed both photographs to a number in France and then used the telephone on the desk. "Hello, it's Anton." He spoke Serbian. "I sent you two faxes, this man came to the shop asking for Vesic, said he is a salesman from Portland, Oregon. I gave you the name and two phone numbers he left and his license plate. He's been to the port and knows about the bank. I'm sure he'll come back. What do you want me to do?"

— "Close the shop, lock everything up, go someplace you've never been to for a week, call this number everyday at this time. If I have something for you I'll tell you. Make sure you stay where I can reach you, I'll be asking you to get us hardware." Novak hang up and turned to Vlad. "You're going back to America, Chicago, it's cold there, take warm clothes, pack only a carry-on, find your belt, I'll give you dollars, take American credit cars, take the train to Paris, fly direct to Chicago. Make copies of the fax from Anton and take the copies with you, that's your mark, call me from the train and I'll let you know where you'll find your mark. Leave now. Take the TGV. Make sure you have your Blackberry with you."

Vlad was on the Lyon-Paris TGV late that evening and paid near two thousand dollars for a non-stop round trip ticket to Chicago departing at noon Wednesday. He arrived at O'Hare International Airport at three in the afternoon Chicago time, rented a Chrysler and checked in at the Airport Marriott. An hour later Novak briefed him about his assignment.

John telephoned Gene Kazmierski as he was leaving Muskegon. "You called, Gene."

— "I did. How did it go in Muskegon?"

— "Not sure. Vesic was not in Muskegon. He was there two weeks ago and won't be back until next June. He's got a shipment of car parts going to Marseille, France, via Philadelphia in two weeks. His office in Muskegon is a gun shop and the guy there did not cooperate. I'm on my way back to Chicago, I'll come see you tomorrow."

— "Do that. Donna wants you to bring Sergeant Mackenzie for dinner at the house Friday night." John went silent. "You there? Listen, the attorney we picked at Jack's house is out on bail. We could not charge him with breaking an entry because he has a key and is in the security company's list. He can't be charged with theft because he did not steal anything, so all we were left with is cutting the seals. The District Attorney had no way to make a connection to the plants. First offence, out on bail, he may not even get a trial. We checked the guy's alibi for the day of Jack's death, he was at his father's restaurant in Cicero between seven-thirty and past eleven, with a dozen witnesses. He's clean there. Tell me about the dinner, Carol is a great gal." John remained silent. "Shit, Johnny, everybody knows, what's the big deal?"

— "Dinner on Friday OK. I'll be at your office tomorrow after lunch."

The call from Monty DeSimone came at dinner time. The big Christmas party will be the coming Saturday, tuxedo optional, dark suit mandatory, invitation for John's date impossible. On Thursday John moved back to Patrick's house as the furor with the marihuana plants had subsided and in the afternoon John drove to see Gene and did some shopping. Carol was busy with work so it was not until Friday night, dinner at Gene's, that John saw Carol. It was a hell of an accomplishment to persuade Carol that attending the Christmas party at Taylor Manufacturing Industries was work and that there was no possible way to get an invitation for her.

John was getting dressed when Gianni DiRenzo telephoned. "John, listen good. Some character is following you, we made the guy, a foreigner, drives a black Chrysler, stays at the Airport Marriott, I have people I know there, we've got him covered. If you want we'll pick him up. In the meantime be careful, don't get in situations that the guy can get ahead of us. Keep your phone open, watch your battery."

— "How do you know somebody is following me?"

— "Cause I have two of my people covering your rear. I don't know what kind of shit you stepped on but you did. Just watch where you go, stay in public, please don't go to no alleys."

— "Thanks, Gianni."

Monty DeSimone arrived in a black Cadillac dressed like a movie star. He stayed at Patrick's for one drink and the two of them left for the party. The drive to Taylor Manufacturing Industries took three-quarters of an hour going west and all the time John kept his eye on the mirror on his side trying to identify the two cars following him but had no success.

As Monty drove closer to Taylor Manufacturing Industries John saw police cars parked on the side of the road and a multitude of vehicles ahead of them. A young man dressed all in black with a red vest approached the driver's window and offered to valet the car. "John, if you're armed leave your weapon in the trunk. You'll never make it through security here with a weapon, this place is for all practical purposes a federal institution." Holster, pistol and two magazines went into the safety of Monty's trunk. A golf car drove the two to the gate from where they moved slowly through magnetometers and observing guards. Twenty minutes later they were inside.

Taylor Manufacturing Industries facility is large and resembles a detention center; high concrete walls and observation towers at the corners. Inside the gate a large paved area, now with a red carpet running from the entrance to a large tent obviously set up for the party. To the right of the tent a three-story building with all the lights on and signs reading 'Office / Laboratory'. Behind and to the left of the tent warehouse-type buildings separated from the outside walls by a twenty-foot wide paved fire lane, nobody's land, lit by mercury lights in high posts next to the wall. John noticed two guards with dogs.

— "This is the only entrance and exit, for people and vehicles, no other way in or out. There are escape gates along the wall in case of a fire. The guards working today are from a security agency and very few compared to a normal day, the everyday guards are attending the party with their families. The regulars are ex-military people, you'll meet some at the party. This is basically a federal institution housing a private company. When a truck arrives to make a delivery a guard is assigned to the truck full time. The only shipments out of here are for Uncle Sam and they are made in Army trucks operated by Army personnel. You can't take a box of matches out of this place."

— "Tell me again, What is that they make here?"

— "Taylor has three contracts, the main contract that results in two-thirds of the gross and half of their profits is the manufacturing of a synthetic explosive, if you're familiar with Syntex or C-4 this is the same only that a lot more powerful, safer to handle and with a cost of production fifteen percent lower. They call it SA-286, the name has no meaning that I know. They also have a contract for manufacturing rocket propelled grenades, or RPG's, that are more expensive that those made by the Chinese or the Russians but with a longer range; this is not a big-margin item because RPG's can be made by anybody. That contract runs two more years and Jack advised Taylor that he should stop making RPG's and should concentrate on what gives larger gross and a better percentage. The third contract is for smart bombs, laser-guided bombs, I know nothing about them except that the profit is obscene and that they have no competition at their level of sophistication. Listen, I'll introduce you to a few people I know but after that I've got to go to work, I'll spend my time with their comptroller and a couple of other big wheels. You'll be on your own, meet the Governor, get a picture."

— "And Julia."

— "We'll meet Julia, she'll be busy but I'll introduce you. Julia's company is doing the catering, this is their biggest event of the year. See the trucks that look like UPS vans, those are Julia's, and the yellow Ryder trucks are rented for the party, there'll be feeding twelve hundred people here." They entered the large tent, it was very bright. A band was playing a Glenn Miller tune, easily thirty musicians on the stage. Nobody was dancing, perhaps too early. The Governor was supposed to arrive at ten. The tent was entered at the middle of one of the long sides, the music stage directly in front of the entrance. More than three hundred people were in the tent already, many standing in front of one of the many buffet tables and bars arranged along the perimeter. More people at the bars than at the food tables, it was early yet. At the right end of the tent there was an entrance to a smaller tent. "That's where the big wheels will have a sit down dinner, everybody has access to mingle but I'm sure they don't want the commoners to stay too long. The table seats are pre-assigned, I'm afraid you and me don't qualify as big wheels, but we'll stroll in later on so I can introduce you to our hosts."

The two carried their drinks to one of the many waist-high round tables with no seats near one of the bars and joined three couples discussing the food and planning their photographs with the Governor. The three men worked in the manufacturing plant and none of the women worked there, not a word said about work. Monty introduced himself as an outside consultant and John as his guest, and said he was hoping to meet the guys from accounting and one of the men pointed to a group four tables to their left. Monty went for two glasses of Champagne and took John with him to meet those he wanted to charm, introducing himself as an accounts manager at McAllister & Moyer and everybody from accounting recognized the name. Monty displayed a great deal of humility and confided that his firm was doing everything they could to become Taylor's outside consultant and, without being too obvious a salesman, related all the virtues of his firm. The men at the table were talking about the January audit.

— "The Army people will go over every shred of paper and e-mails and God knows what. They'll keep us till nine o'clock everyday for three weeks. I guess they'll be looking at our costs so they can squeeze us when is time for a new contract."

Monty was very dexter finding out what each man did and made all of them feel good and gave everybody his card and said that he would see each one again soon.

— "You're a good salesman Monty."

— "I have to be, my job depends on it. Let's grab another bubbly and let's go see the bosses, if we wait too long all the big wheels will be there and they won't have time for us little people." The band was playing 'String of Pearls' when the two entered the smaller tent. There were about thirty round tables with six chairs to a table, and the service was porcelain with three sets of utensils and three glasses with very long stems. It pays to be a big wheel. "The blonde in the black dress with no straps is Julie, the man to her right is her father."

— "No mother?"

— "I hear that Julie's mother is very sick, used to be in charge of something important in the office but I can't remember what. What I've heard is that the lady is either in the hospital or home in bed, and very ill." Monty led the way threading around the tables and Julie saw him when they were three tables away.

— "Hey sailor, how're you doing? You look so-o elegant, come say hello to my dad." Julia has the soft look and the refined mannerisms that one associates with royalty or with Hollywood's leading ladies, thin and not so tall, very light blue eyes and rather white skin, with short blond hair exposing a diamond on each ear lobe, in a low-cut long dress of black silk with no straps, smiling, smiling, smiling. "Dad, say hello to Monty."

— "Mr. Taylor, I'm happy to see you, thanks for the invitation, this is a great event, I do appreciate."

— "Monty, it's always a pleasure to see you. Used to see you more at the club, now you're always working. Who's your friend?" Mr. Taylor had white hair cut very short and the same light blue eyes as his daughter, darker skin and few wrinkles, appeared to be fit. "Come sit with us for a moment, soon I'll have to entertain the Generals and you don't need to worry about entertaining my people, your contract will be delivered as soon as the lawyers are done. How's that for good news?"

— "Well, you've made more than my day Mr. Taylor, you made my year. I do appreciate it." Monty was all smiles. "Mr. Taylor, this is John O'Rourke, Jack O'Rourke's father, I took the liberty of bringing John to your party." Monty was giving Mr. Taylor time to register who John was.

Mr. Taylor had ceased to listen to Monty and had turned his head towards John. "I can't tell you how much I liked your son, not just I but all of us who met Jack. Please accept my condolences, I'm well aware that words don't mean much but I have to tell you that I'm very sorry for your loss. Jack was a fine young man, he helped us a great deal too. But Monty can explain that to you better. I hope you're able to cope. Is Mrs. O'Rourke here too?"

— "I'm afraid I lost my wife many years ago. I thank you for your sympathy, I wasn't too much of a father for Jack and I'm suffering not only his death but my guilt as well. A life lived wrong, I suppose, can't be undone." John surprised himself revealing that much of himself, Mr. Taylor projected a warmth that made you want to be close to him. "We don't want to take all your time Mr. Taylor, I'm sure you have many to see, maybe I'll come back to get my picture with the Governor. And an awful lot of thanks for having me at your party, it's a treat for me." John shook hands with Mr. Taylor and Julie stood on her toes to kiss John on both cheeks.

— "I'd like to meet the man who's your comptroller, I brought with me a sheet of paper Jack left for me that I wish to show him." John placed the palm of his right hand on the left side of his chest."

It was Julie who answered. "I'll find Ben Piesecki and I'll bring him to you."

— "And how will you find me?"

— "It'll be easy, I'll check what direction the women are turning to. I've got a little bit of work to do first to see that all is set up right, then I'll come for you. Do you dance?"

More people had entered the smaller tent and the larger tent was crowded. The band was playing 'American Patrol'. The bar to the right of the band stand seemed the least crowded and Monty led in that direction. "You made a splash there, Julie was more enthused than I've ever seen her. You never answered if you dance, I hope you do, your son was a swell dancer." John had not heard anybody say 'swell' since Jimmy Carter's time. John let Monty explain the virtues of his firm to an audience of office personnel and walked outside the large tent, there was still a line of people on the red carpet leading to the tent. John walked towards the office building, a white structure with much glass in the front and side. Inside the building the catering people had set up store and waiters were coming into the building with empty carts and left pushing full carts the opposite way. Boxes with food and liquor were rolled out of large vans with 'La Bonne Vie' painted in white letters on the side, Julie's company trucks. How many boxes to feed twelve hundred people?, How many bottles? John attempted to do the math but gave up. How many children in China could be fed? What was the sense of all this? A celebration of Christmas by the world's leading experts in bomb making, the same ones that pride themselves in creating the most efficient killing compound. There was something Kafkaesque is this proceedings, a grotesque display of wrong values that none of the attendants had taken the time to evaluate. John walked towards the silver and blue helicopter resting in the center of a large circle painted in white on the black asphalt, but could not get too close as the two guards moved in his direction with a stern look in their faces.

— "I'll stay with Champagne please." John walked around the tables until he sighted Monty, who was standing very close to a tuxedo-clad tall young stud with black wavy hair down to his shoulders. John kept moving and went to a food table where a young attendant served him octopus salad and ahi tuna, that he took to one of the stand-up tables with three couples more or less his age and listened to them talk well about their company and praise Mr. Taylor. The same young lady served him a plate of mango and papaya slices out of an array of all the fruits known to man and John walked to a stand-up table with four men with military haircuts and two women that appeared to be dates and introduced himself as Lieutenant O'Rourke of the Chicago Police Department and a marine; one of the men was a marine and they exchanged Camp Pendleton stories. Nearly one hundred twenty men and women work in the security force, three eight-hour shifts, the latest in electronics and an attitude that says 'we can do no wrong'. No personal vehicles ever enter the facility, not even Mr. Taylor's, no carry-on lunches since the cafeteria is free. Personnel walk through magnetometers as they come to work and as they leave the premises and are subjected to random searches. They even search Mr. Taylor's helicopter every day.

The Governor arrived at ten sharp and John waited for the big wheels to finish their dinners before going for a photo with the Gov but the line was too long and John desisted. The band was back playing 'Always' when Julie whispered "Do you wanna dance with me?" in John's ear. John did.

They danced to 'Old Skokian', 'Amapola' and 'Star Dust' with their bodies pressed together and their cheeks touching and walked outside for fresh air listening to 'Chattanooga Choo Choo'. "Your food is wonderful, I've eaten so many things I like and never run into."

— "Well, you'll have to stick with me and you'll eat well. Our left overs are more than what five families with twenty children buy for a full week. What's left from one function can not be used elsewhere."

— "You throw it away?"

— "Oh no, the help takes as much as they can carry, that's one of their perks, the rest we truck to institutions in Evanston that feed the old and the poor. We get lots of Brownie points from that. We cook and make everything we serve, the desserts too." Julie was proud of her business. They walked slowly, towards the office building, Julie grabbed John's arm with her left hand. "I met your son, and his friend too, they came to Monty's boat a couple of times, I liked Jack very much, he was wonderful. I find it difficult to talk about death, I guess I'm afraid of it, maybe because my mother is close to it, she's very ill." Julie changed subjects. "I heard you live in Florida. Where?" They made small talk and went back to the big tent. A small group was filling in for the big band and the music was two steps too quick for John, so they went for coffee and chocolate cake and walked into the smaller tent to sit at an empty table.

— "I lost sight of Monty."

— "Yes you did, Monty left with one of my greeters before we danced. I told him I'll drive you home."

A man in a tuxedo approached the table and sat next to Julie. Medium frame, five-ten, hundred-seventy pounds, dark hair cut short parted on the left, mid-sixties, glasses, no facial hair, manicured hands. "This is Ben Piesecki, he's my Dad's comptroller, you said you wanted to meet him."

— "I do, pleased to meet you Mr. Piesecki, I'm Jack O'Rourke's father." They shook hands and John was surprised by Mr. Piesecki's very strong handshake; that pleased John, good sign. "I have a paper that was John's, a spreadsheet with some writing on its back. You may be able to make something out of it."

John pulled the folded sheet from his inside pocket, unfolded it and handed it to Mr. Piesecki with Jack's handwriting facing up.

— "I'm very sorry about your son, I worked with Jack on and off for three months. Jack was very pleasant to work with, and a good accountant. Hard worker too. He helped our company a great deal, uncovered something very ugly that we're in the process of correcting. We would have been awfully embarrassed with our client had not been for Jack. The company will turn stronger thanks to Jack. Let me see." Mr. Piesecki slid his bifocals to the middle of his nose and turned the page over to read the spreadsheet.

— "These are the weights, this is the heart of our problem."

— "I'm really interested in the other side, there is a handwritten note from Jack. Some figures and a name, Stephen Vesic. What do you make of it?"

— "The numbers are the weights totaled."

— "I care about the handwritten part, Stephen Vesic, the key." Piesecki was sidetracked and John was letting his impatience show.

— "I don't know about the key but Vesic is an export agent we used years ago for a shipment to Europe, samples for a prospective client. Vesic took care of the documentation for us. That was, I can tell you exactly, six years ago this coming January. Never did business with Vesic again."

— "You sure?"

— "I'm the comptroller, Mr. O'Rourke, I've been with the firm for twenty-nine years, I'm in charge here, I run a very tight ship, I earn my penny. I'm sure I'm sure." Piesecki was testy.

— "You know how to reach this Vesic?"

— "No, but I'm sure we have his address in our database. We store all documents forever. Army regulation. The Army auditors have a joke: 'You may dispose of a document only after you make five copies of it.' I'll have Vesic's address and telephone number for you Monday morning, say ten o'clock. Telephone me or I can e-mail you, your choice." John took the sheet from Mr. Piesecki, folded it and put it back in his inside pocket.

— "I'll telephone your office Monday at ten. Thank you for your help, it's been good meeting you." Piesecki had said weights, What weights? John thought better not to ask, he thought it was wiser not to reveal his ignorance.

Chapter 10
Julie

THE GOVERNOR HAD LEFT long ago and the last group of guests was filing through the gate, few cars remained in the parking lot. In the tents there was a flurry of activities, all tables had been cleaned and the food that was left had been removed in carts. Outside, racks and boxes were being rolled into trucks that moved slowly towards the double gate, each directed by one guard that walked in front of the truck, careful of not approaching the helicopter pad. John counted six trucks that went through the gate and another eight still to be loaded. Julie had said to wait outside. The two guards standing outside had their eyes glued on Julie as she came through the gate, wearing a black coat with large lapels and black gloves. "Sorry, I had to say good night to my Dad and he wanted to talk. I'll make it up for you. Want to come to my boat?"

Julie drove a silver four-door Volvo with tinted windows. "I'm taking you to my boat. We'll have a bottle of bubbly to celebrate that we've met." John was thinking about the two cars that were not following him."

— "I met lots of people, everybody seems to love your father."

— "Dad's really a great guy. He inherited a good business from my grandfather and grew it ten-fold into a great business, and set me up in business too, I did not enjoy working in Dad's company. Our military is better equipped today because of Dad, the Generals love him too." Julie drove fast. "Dad's having a hard time, he and my Mom have been married for forty-six years and have spent every day together, literally, every single day, I'm not exaggerating. My Mom used to work in the company, started as a typist and worked her way up to be the head of quality control. My Mom is very ill, she may not live to

86

see the new year. And suffering too. Other than work, Dad spends all of his time with my Mom."

— "Was that your father's helicopter?"

— "Yes, Dad lives on the waterfront, his building has a pad. For you and me it's an hour and a half ride with good traffic, Dad gets to his office in fifteen minutes. Dad would trade the helicopter and his whole company for Mom being healthy." John understood, he had lived through that.

— "I didn't get what Piesecki said about the weights."

— "Your son compared the weight of certain components they use at the plan to the weight of the final product and there was a deficiency, most likely it is an error in record keeping. You have to realize that this place is run so tight that you could not lose a pencil. But if your son had not found the error, the Army auditors would have found it and it would have been an embarrassment to my father. The Army takes record-keeping very seriously, and security too."

— "You don't think the weights may be related to Jack's death, Do you? Somebody stealing from your Dad's company thinking that Jack found out who he was? Until today I had not paid any attention to the numbers on the spreadsheet, I only cared for this Vesic character."

— "I don't know what to tell you, but you should speak to my Dad. Jack told my Dad there is a thief and Dad will see that they find him. It's only a matter of time."

— "Your boat is named Julie, right?"

— "Yes, siree, my Dad named after me, though he never calls me Julie, to my Mom and Dad I'm Little Babushka. No matter how many years I pile on, how many meals I serve, I'm still Little Babushka." Julie made the turn and drove towards the waterfront. "You'll like the boat, everybody does, every year we do a cruise to nowhere the week before Christmas, this year you'll be my personal guest. We go out for two days and two nights, it's fun. I cater that too. The crew is getting Julie ready, the day before the cruise they'll take her out to test the engines and everything else."

— "And when is the cruise?"

— "Let me see, it's already Sunday, a week from tomorrow, we'll sail at seven on Monday evening to dine at ten, and we'll be back late Wednesday evening. We have a French menu, every dish is Provencal, you'll love it."

— "You'll have to tell me how to dress."

Ten minutes to go to reach the Yacht Club and John did not see cars behind them. "Honey, do me two favors, one, turn off your telephone, and two, slide down in your seat, I like it better if the guard does not see you so I can preserve my virtuous image." John turned off his telephone and slid down in his seat so his head was touching the middle of the backrest, which really did not matter since the guard recognized Julie's Volvo and waved her through. Julie drove close to the pier to park her Volvo and they walked to her yacht. Seen from below, Julie's Julie seemed to be ten-story high and a city-block long.

From the main deck they entered the saloon that had a good-size bar and a number of sofas and stuffed chairs arranged in groups. "Let's go up to the sun deck, there's a hot tub, we'll skinny dip, we'll see Monty's boat from there, I'm sure he and Terry are having fun. Don't worry about the crew, they stay under deck and they're sure sleeping by now." Julie let her coat slip on the floor and took her shoes and gloves off. "Or would you rather see my cabin? Your choice." And she walked to a refrigerator behind the front bar and pulled a bottle of Dom Perignon and two fluted glasses. "Will you please open this?" And handed the bottle to John who immediately started fighting the wire. "Want to know about my boat, I'll give you the short version. Designed by Stefano Natucci, Stefano is the Christian Dior of yachts, hundred-and-fifty feet, six staterooms, can do fifteen knots and can go four thousand miles, a crew of three. How's that?"

— "How many gallons of fuel?"

— "Everybody's question. Seventy thousand liters, that's fifteen thousand gallons of diesel. You can go around Lake Michigan several times on that."

John half-filled the flutes and handed one to Julie. "It must be nice. Way out of my league." John had finished his glass of bubbly when they heard a phone ring.

— "That's the land line, I wonder who it may be." Julie disappeared through a door on the side of the front bar and came back irritated. "It's the guard, so much for my virtue. There is a detective parked at the guard house who says there is an emergency, that Captain Somebody needs you right now. You better go. Here." Julie wrote on a paper napkin. "Call me tomorrow, I'd like you to take me out."

John recognized Carol's Mazda parked next to the guard house. "What's the emergency?"

— "The emergency is that you were on that boat to bed that skinny bitch, that's the emergency. Listen, I've heard in the department all about your adventures, how many you've laid and what a stud you used to be. That's not going be the case with us, that bullshit is over. I'll be loyal to you and you'll be loyal to me. It's about time you grow up." And Carol broke up crying. "You son of a bitch, I'm in love with you, Why do you do this to me?" And kept crying.

— "Carol, you're wrong, we've got to talk." It was ten minutes to five on Sunday morning. The streets were empty, John could see no cars behind them. They arrived at Patrick's house before six and sat in the den, John made coffee. "Do you have the picture? Are we clear? Use Patrick's computer and buy me the ticket, use this credit card, first class, one way to Orlando leaving this afternoon to arrive before seven, please print me a boarding pass, I want to go straight to the gate. I'll drive back from Orlando, will be back Thursday, no later than Friday." John went upstairs trying not to make noises but Patrick was up and met him in his room.

— "You guys all right?, We can hear everything from our bedroom, we're above the den."

— "We're fine. Things are coming to a head, I can't tell you now but I will later when it won't get you in trouble. I'm flying back to Orlando, I'll be back at the end of the week. All right if I stay here again?" John packed only a few things in his carry-on.

— "This is your house John."

— "Thanks, Patrick, I'll leave my things as they are. I took two bath towels with me. I need my bag to look full."

— "Why?"

— "You don't want to know."

Carol was in front of Patrick's computer when John came back from upstairs. "Having trouble?" John checked the time, ten past ten, he still needed to go to Monty's car for his weapon.

— "Hold on, you're booked with American leaving O'Hare at three forty-five, flight fifteen-twentysix, have to be at the airport at two-thirty. I'm trying to print your boarding pass."

John said his goodbyes and took his carry-on to his rental car after he spoke to Monty to let him know he was leaving for Orlando and arranged to retrieve his weapon, they would meet in the parking lot at the Yacht Club at half past noon. "Follow me, I have to return this car and then we've got to drive to the Yacht Club, I need to see Monty for a minute." After a few blocks John telephoned DiRenzo.

— "You said you wanted to help me, here is your chance. I'm flying American to Orlando at three-fortyfive, flight fifteen-twentysix, write it down, have your main guy meet me at the gate no later than three-ten. He'll have to buy a ticket to somewhere and get a boarding pass so he can walk pass security. I'll let your guy know what I'll need and what you need to do. I'll be back in Chicago before Friday, I'll need your people ready to go on Friday and they may have to stay with me for a day or two. Call me back to confirm your man will meet me at the gate."

The rental car was returned, John's semi-automatic and clips retrieved and secured in the Mazda glove compartment, the confirmation from DiRenzo was received. On the way to O'Hare John's phone rang, 'Please God, make it not be Julie'. It was one of DiRenzo's men. "Say, this is Lefty, I work for Mr. DiRenzo, I'm ten cars behind you, the guy that follows you is five cars behind you, black Chrysler, on the inside lane. What do you want me to do with him?"

— "Nothing, don't do anything, I'll lose him in the airport, he won't be able to follow me, he's got no time. Who's going to meet me at the gate?"

— "Pauley is there already, Mr. DiRenzo said you know him. You sure about the guy? He registered at the Marriott as Vlad Tarasov from France."

— "Let him lose, he's no threat, I'll handle him. But tell me what he looks like, so I know."

— "Tall and very thin with a big nose, so far every day he's worn a black leather jacket. Ugly looking character, sticks out, long black hair to the shoulders and a black moustache. Sometimes wears a baseball cap, sometimes sun glasses."

Carol cut in front of several cars and crossed through three lanes to get to the outside lane and stopped the car thirty feet pass the end of Terminal Three, John got out and walked back to the terminal, jogged to the secure area, at least a hundred fifty people in line waiting to go through security, only four ladies in the first class cue, John went through security in a few minutes and hurried to the end of Concourse H to find his gate. It'd be impossible for his follower, even if he abandoned his car on the street, to find him.

John saw Pauley standing near the gate and took time to call Julie but had no answer. John left her a message that he had to leave for Orlando in a hurry, he lied that there was a package from Jack that had arrived last week and said he'd be back in Chicago on time for the cruise."

The meeting with Pauley was brief, Pauley said all can be arranged, no sweat, and called John's cellular so this would have his number, and asked John if he wanted one of his men fly to Orlando with him. John declined.

Vlad had realized too late that the Mazda had crossed the three lanes to its right and kept driving straight without a second thought, he knew where to find his mark. He parked on the shoulder and telephoned Novak.

— "Return your car and wait. I'll call you back." By the time Novak returned the call forty minutes later Vlad had dismantled his two pistols and had distributed the parts and clips in garbage bins in the rental agency and saved some to dispose of in front of Terminal Three. The ammo he put in a plastic bag and dropped it in the trash can in the rental agency's men's room. At five minutes before six Vlad was sitting in first class in American Flight nineteen-sixtyseven that would arrive in Orlando at ten o'clock that night.

John landed in Orlando at six-fifty and rented a four-wheel drive SUV with tinted glass windows and a GPS system. "Rick, you gonna be home tonight? I'd like to come over and stay for the night, just got here from Chicago and I haven't slept since Friday and I have a friend in my house entertaining somebody's wife, can't go there until the morning. All right with you?" John drove around the block twice to make sure nobody was following him and let his SUV with the valet in front of Rick Nixon's spiffy apartment house, waited until the Concierge cleared him with Rick and rode the elevator that serves the penthouses. They shared stone crabs and a lobster a client of Rick's had sent from Joe's Crabs in Miami Beach and drank a beer made by a mini-brewer downtown as they watched the Heat play the Lakers. John fell asleep on the sofa as soon as Koby had scored twenty points, moved to a bed at midnight, and was showered, shaved and dressed at eight sharp. Rick was already gone.

At one of the two gates that provide access to John's gated community, instead of going through the resident's lane John stopped next to the guardhouse. "Randy, I need a favor, I'm in a screwed-up situation and there is a reporter hounding me. I need to know when he gets here, please tell your buddies too, I don't want this guy to surprise me and start taking photos. He'll be here today, tomorrow or Wednesday and most likely he'll say he's looking at the real estate or some bullshit like that, so he can get in."

— "Don't worry, we won't let him in. What does the guy look like?"

— "No, no, no. I want you to let him in, I'll talk to him, I just don't want photos. If I don't talk to him soon he'll pester me forever." John was sure that by now all the guards knew what had happened, Jack's death, the plants. "White male, tall, skinny, ugly, black hair long to the shoulder, black mustache. Let him in but telephone me as soon as he goes through the gate."

— "No sweat, will do. And John, sorry about your loss. Too bad what happened to your son."

It was eight blocks on winding streets and three turns to get to John's house. When he arrived, instead of going onto the driveway, John parked across the street and called the Police Department. "Listen, I just came back home from a trip and I think I saw somebody inside my house, nobody is supposed to be there. Can you send a couple of officers."

— "Just stay in your car or better yet keep driving, don't go too far, a patrol car will be there in five minutes, I have your number, an officer will call you. Don't repeat don't go into the house. Wait for us to get there. Give me your address."

— "I know what not to do. I was a policeman in Chicago for twenty-five years. Magnolia Drive, nine-eighteen, white house, one story, there is a big magnolia tree on the left side if you're facing the house. I'll be sitting inside a dark blue Suburban across the street."

The patrol car arrived in seven minutes, parked alongside John's SUV, they spoke a few words and John gave the officer his key. "All right if we take Max inside the house? Max will sniff the intruder if there is one." The officers parked the patrol car in front of John's house and walked through the white gate with a large grey dog on a leash in front of them and drew their pistols as they reached the house, both were wearing Kevlar vests. They came out in fifteen minutes. "Clean as a whistle, we looked everywhere, under beds, closets, checked inside your cupboard too in case the intruder is a midget. If anybody was there, Max would have found him too, all doors and windows are secure. You used to be a cop?"

— "Detective in Chicago, twenty-five years."

— "You …, You lost your son recently?"

— "Yeah, it's me alright."

— "We're very sorry." The officer was uneasy, "Well, you may go in, your house is clean."

Vlad telephoned Novak as the wheels touched the tarmac and received his instructions, he wrote down an address in Tampa and used the map finder in his Blackberry to figure out how to get there and how long it would take. He rented a black Cadillac that smelled of new car and followed the road to Interstate Four and then drove west to Tampa. Two hours later Vlad checked-in at a Red Roof Inn following a burger and fries and was in bed shortly after one. At nine he checked out, drank coffee in the lobby and followed the directions in his Cadillac's GPS to find the Viking Gun Shop on Liberty Road, not in Tampa but in Brandon, directly east of Tampa. Vlad parked in front of the entrance and waited, Novak had said they open at ten; he had nine minutes to go over his plan. There was only one other store in the small strip center, something to do with bail bonds, and no other vehicles in the parking lot. At five minutes pass ten a silver pickup truck arrived followed by a red Ford Mustang. The pickup truck continued to the end of the strip and disappeared behind the building and the red Mustang parked several slots away from Vlad's Cadillac. An old man wearing jeans, boots and a white tee-shirt got out of the Mustang, walked quickly to the entrance door and waited for it to be opened from the inside. He entered the store without turning or looking towards Vlad's Cadillac.

Vlad waited a few minutes and walked to the door, it was a heavy steel door, and it was locked. Before Vlad could knock on the door, this opened towards the inside and a voice asked "Who sent you?"

— "Anton."

A hand appeared from behind the door made into a fist and holding a gray cloth. "Here, put this on, I don't want to see your face. Come in." It was a gray hood that came all the way to Vlad's shoulders but did not cover all his hair, the kind of hood duck hunters might use in the winter, possibly so the ducks can not identify them. Vlad pulled the hood down to have the opening at his eyes's level, it made his face hot. The old man was walking in front of Vlad, facing away from him. "I have what you need and have a fax for you too, three sheets. I need to see the money. Are you covered?"

— "I have the money. I put the hood on."

— "I need to see the money first, six thousand dollars. Now, see the holes on the wall in the back, that's where my partner is holding a hunting rifle, dead shot that he is." The old man walked back and locked the door, three locks,

93

top, middle and bottom. "This door and the one on the back wall are the only ways out. Sometimes young punks think they can rob us with our own weapons and try to do stupid things. It don't work. My buddy will be on you every second you're here. Understood?"

— "I did not come here to rob you, old man. I'll need to take my belt out to show you the money, make sure your buddy does not do something stupid either." Vlad unzipped his leather jacket and laid it on a table covered with piles of camouflaged pants and shirts, and pulled a cotton belt from under his shirt, opened a pocket and took several thousand-dollar bills, counted six and handed them to the old man. "Six thousand dollars, that's what you said. Let me see the pistol."

The old man counted six bills, folded them and put them in his jeans pocket. "On the glass counter, what Anton asked for, a twenty-two caliber Browning, twelve rounds in the clip, it comes with two clips, I can get you more but it may take me a few days. The pistol has very good balance, it's light on the hand, the sights are true and it's been cleaned and oiled. I'll give you oil and cloth for you to take. Walk with me, I have a gallery in the back, you can try the weapon to forty feet. I'll give you a box with one hundred rounds, no charge."

— "I'll need something else, nine-millimeter, a Glock."

— "I can give you a used pistol for another six grand."

— "Let me see those two in the counter." Vlad was looking through the glass top a counter displaying three or four dozen nine-millimeter and .45 caliber semi-automatic pistols.

— "I can't sell you any of those. You need a license for those and they can be traced to me. No can do. I have the same item, two years old, perfect condition and can't be traced, that's why it's six grand and not a grand and a half like those under the glass. Come walk with me." The shooting gallery was no more than six foot wide, dark, with a small table covered with green felt stained with oil. There was a smell of dust and dampness in the air. The target was a white square cardboard glued over plywood with one black circle four inches in diameter and another two thin black circles each two inches larger, fixed on two metal strips attached to a sliding mechanism that allowed the target to be pulled forward and reach the small table.

— "Set the target at ten feet." Vlad waited, the old man pressed the button on the table and the target moved slowly forward to reach one of the many white lines painted on the right wall. Vlad took the clip out, removed two rounds and put them back in, pushed the one on the top with his thumb and noticed that the clip was not full, placed the clip back, pulled the slide back and released it to load the first round and held the pistol pointing down in front of the table, took a deep breath, let the air go and took half a breath, raised the pistol to be level and shot in quick sequence until the clip was empty. Eight rounds. The old man brought the target to reach the table, eight shots inside the four-inch diameter circle. "Let me try the Glock, put twelve rounds in the clip, same target, twenty-five feet." The old man took the Glock's clip out and added six rounds, and moved the target back to the twenty-five foot line. Vlad went through the same routine and shot twelve rounds in bursts of two." All shots inside the second circle, twelve shots inside a six-inch diameter target. Vlad enjoyed showing off his skill.

— "Here you have another six thousand. Please empty all clips and wipe all rounds, the clips and all parts you touched, I don't want to carry your signature with me." Each of the pistols was wrapped in cloth, two magazines for each, one hundred rounds for each pistol went into a small orange nylon bag with Adidas in blue letters on both sides. "I need a jacket, leather is too heavy for here. Size large." The two walked back into the store and the old man found a dark blue waterproof jacket and four white tee-shirts. "Thanks, Can you tell me where to find a barber?"

Vlad all his hair cut and his head shaved; the mustache went too. From the barber Vlad drove to a sporting goods store where he purchased a back pack, a music player with earphones, running shorts and shirt, a warm up suit and a pair of running shoes. He dressed in shorts and a shirt and wore the warm up suit on top. Vlad stopped at a fast food place and studied the three sheets Novak had faxed him, a map of John's gated community showing the street names and the gate houses and a larger-scale map showing a section of the community with John's house in the center identified by a heavy circle.

Vlad arrived at Paradise Gardens at half past four in the afternoon and asked the guard if he could look around, that he and his wife were looking for a safe place with a golf course. Fabiana let Vlad in and since the guy had neither long black hair nor a mustache Fabiana did not call John. Vlad drove his Cadillac around the winding streets until he felt he was familiar with the layout and was sure he could get out of Paradise Gardens safely without getting lost in a mace of streets that look all the same. Vlad drove from the mark's house to the gate twice, three and a half minutes at slow speed, stop signs at every corner, a few people waiting for the sun to go down to start their barbeques, an old lady gardening. Vlad parked the Cadillac two blocks from the mark's house, put the keys in the back pack where he had the 22-caliber pistol and an extra clip, took off his warm up suit and started jogging away from the mark's house listening to the BeeGees, he'd do a mile to work out a sweat before getting to the mark. Vlad left the Glock and his cotton belt inside the orange nylon bag that he placed on the back seat, hidden under the warm up jacket.

John was getting tired of being outside. At each of the windows he had placed one of the motion detectors he had purchased at the Home Depot on his way in that would ring if the glass was touched, and the rear door was locked and secured with a dead bolt, also had a motion detector plus a hard rubber wedge underneath that would impede its opening. He'd do the same with the front door before he retired for the night. John had watered all the plants in the front lawn, which was not needed as there is a sprinkler system, had trimmed the plants twice, had re-nailed the supports of the new palm trees, had trimmed the lower branches of the big magnolia, had washed and waxed his red Carrera and finally had pulled out the cart with the battery charger and was now in the process of cleaning the brass terminals with steel wool. John had uncoiled the heavy cables earlier and these were laying on the driveway next to two lengths of chain that John had washed in soap and water earlier and were now hot on the concrete pavement. Late afternoon in mid-December and the Florida sun was still hot. It was five-thirty and the guards had not called, John did expect Vlad to come during the day, he'd be less noticeable than during the night, when the guards patrol the street, not to stop characters like Vlad but because of teenagers jumping the wall and doing mischief to the trees, sometimes robbing the garages. The Vlads of this world do not come to Paradise Gardens.

John noticed the jogger one block away coming towards him at a fast pace, he had brought a low stool from the kitchen and was sitting on it with his back to the garage laboring the steel wool on the brass terminals trying to remove the green oxide that did not want to leave after being there for so long. The jogger stopped at the end of the driveway, young man, tall and thin but no long hair and no mustache. John smiled at the young man and went back to the terminals. The jogger turned to his right to face John but did not walk into the driveway. John had a Kevlar vest under his tan long-sleeve shirt and a semi-automatic in his shorts's right pocket; the jogger was wearing blue shorts with no room to hide anything and a yellow shirt with no sleeves tight to his body. If the jogger were to reach for his backpack John would have his pistol in his right hand long before being in any danger. The jogger bent to press both hands on the back of his legs just above his knees, exposing his small backpack, and stayed in that position for half a minute before walking four steps onto the driveway. John dropped the steel wool into the bucket and stood up. "Sir, I wonder if you could give me a glass of water, I think I'm dehydrating and I did not bring my bottle. Tap water will do, two big glasses if you can, cold will be great. I'll stay here." The jogger was crouched down half way from the garage to the end of the driveway. John hated people calling him 'Sir'.

— "Sure, I'll get you a pitcher of ice water from the refrigerator. Sit on the stool, give your legs a rest." John walked into the garage on his way to the kitchen and was out of sight when Vlad entered the garage. Vlad had unzipped the top of the back pack and was three steps inside the garage with his right arm bent over his left shoulder reaching for his pistol when he saw John come out from behind the white upright freezer with a pistol in each hand. Vlad had a glimpse of the laser light before the two darts hit his chest and discharged twentysix watts near his hart. John kept his index pulling the trigger of the Taser X26C Stun Gun he carried in his right hand for thirty seconds, Vlad hit the concrete floor with his knees first and then with his face, breaking the bridge of his nose and bleeding. John sat the Taser next to Vlad's right side and moved the semi-automatic to his right pocket. First he tied Vlad's wrists very tight behind Vlad's back, then gave Vlad a ten-second jolt to be safe, closed the garage door and turned the lights on and finally used a second plastic tie around Vlad's ankles. The last touch was to run a length of electric wire through the wrists and ankles ties and pull Vlad's legs up until his ankles were as close to his wrists as they would go. John had to clean the blood on Vlad's mouth before he used one length of gray duct tape around Vlad's mouth and another around his eyes; John rolled Vlad's body onto a sheet of plastic and gave Vlad a third jolt before pulling off his socks and used a pair of scissors to cut off the back pack and all of Vlad's clothes.

John opened the garage door to retrieve the battery charger and the two lengths of chains before he started pulling on the plastic sheet to drag Vlad to the guest bathroom; it took a great deal of pulling to lift Vlad to the edge and then into the tub. One more ten-second jolt and John wrapped one length of chain twice around Vlad's armpits and the other he wrapped around Vlad's knees. He will give Vlad thirty minutes to wake up and evaluate the predicament he was in. John left the bathroom door open and sat on a chair from where he could see the tub. He used the house phone to call Terry McKenna in Boulder, Colorado.

— "Terry, it's Johnny, Howsit going? I'm glad to see you're home working and not wasting your time playing golf. Can't slack on me, I'm counting on you." Terry teaches the use of explosives at the Colorado School of Mines in Golden, Colorado.

— "I'll be done end of the day tomorrow, I made two units, I'll use one as a test. Up in the hills, I'll scare a few buzzards." John and Terry had been friends since their service days, had vacationed with their wives when Maureen was alive, now visited each other from time to time and played golf. "Mary wants you to stay up for dinner, she's got a new candidate for you, this one is younger, real pretty and recently divorced. Be here on Wednesday, tomorrow night if you want to see the test."

— "It'll have to be Wednesday, I'll be flying in, driving out."

— "Good, you can't carry this stuff in an airplane full of people, plus you could not carry it as luggage, at Denver International they X-ray every piece. Anyway, I'm using two fluids, there will be a concentrated explosion first and then a very hot fire, same as would happen with a gas leak only a lot stronger. You'll have to carry the bottles with the fluids in two separate boxes, can't take chances, and you'll have to do a little assembling just before you set it up, nothing complicated. I used regular electrical wires, the glass containers are bottles of orange juice, everything else is plastic that will burn. Instead of a clock I adapted the kind of timer that Jack could have used with his plants, I think I covered every base. There'll nothing left for the insurance guys."

— "Maybe they'll hire you to investigate, you'll make an extra buck."

— "That'll be day. What about Mary's recent discovery? She's nice."

— "Tell Mary I made my own discovery. I'll bring Carol to your house for dinner soon, after all this shit is over. I've got to go Terry, I have a guy waiting for me. See you Wednesday afternoon. I'll call you Tuesday night at home to see how the test went. If you're not there I'll know the test went bad. So long Terry."

— "See you on Wednesday Johnny, take good care."

— "Listen Terry, remember I need forty-eight hours on the timer, this is important, I want to be far away when it goes up, the timer has to be precise, I'll set it up for the afternoon when the neighbors are at work, I don't want to take a chance with people getting hurt."

— "The timer is very accurate, you're paying several hundred bucks for the timer alone. It'll be accurate to one second, it has a digital setting up to sixty hours."

— "Thanks Terry, say hello to Mary."

Chapter 11
Recycling

The back pack had a twenty-two caliber semi-automatic, an extra magazine, Vlad's passport, a Blackberry, two keys with the Cadillac emblem and a wallet with a folded airline ticket, more than ten thousand dollars in cash and several credit cards all in the name of Vlad Tarasov, no driver's license, no notes. Vlad had carried with him all he would need in case he had to take off on foot in a hurry. John spread the back pack contents on the kitchen table and used the house phone to call the guard house; Fabiana answered on the second ring. "It's Johnny O'Rourke, Fabiana. Did you a see a bold guy come in driving a Cadillac?" Fabiana said she did and volunteered that the man drove alone and that he went through the gate at exactly four-thirty-three, she had recorded the time on the log, Was anything the matter? "No, I just want to let you know that Mark will be staying for dinner and that he parked his Cadillac two or three blocks away but is not sure where, as he had trouble finding my house. Don't worry about the Cadillac, we'll go out in my car after dinner and will bring it to the house before it's too late, I know the rules." All John needed to know was that Vlad came in alone. "Don't forget about the guy I'm waiting for, telephone me if you see any strange character, I don't want reporters in my house this late."

John had to ride his bicycle for ten minutes before he saw a black Cadillac parked on Willow Lane, pushed the button in the larger key and saw the Cadillac's head lights blink twice. He searched the trunk first and found only a black leather jacket with empty pockets. On the back seat John found the pants and top of a warm up suit hiding an orange hand bag, and a leather bag with shirts, sweaters, underwear, two pair of sun glasses and a bathroom kit. Inside the orange bag John found a Glock with a full magazine and a round in the chamber, an extra magazine also full and a cotton belt with six compartments that John opened and emptied, forty-eight thousand dollars in thousand-dollar bills, three thousand in hundreds and ten thousand Euros. John took the orange bag and the cotton belt with him and locked the Cadillac.

Vlad was awake and had wiggled his way inside the tub to be leaning on his right side, and was trying to bite into the duct tape on his mouth with no success. John opened the faucet to let cold water run into the tub, making Vlad rotate his body until he laid on his back while keeping his head high and turning from side to side trying to see through the duct tape that covered his eyes. John left to came back minutes later pulling the cart with the battery charger, and left again this time to come back pulling the end of a very thick orange cord that he plugged into the battery charger. On his third trip John brought back the stool he had used outside and opened the drain to empty the tub. John pulled on both chains to rest Vlad's back on the tub and pulled the duct tape from around Vlad's eyes, then moved the battery charger to be next to the tub's edge and connected one of the terminals to the chain around Vlad's armpits and the other to the chain around Vlad's knees. Vlad's eyes opened wide and he had a terrified look on his face. John left the bathroom door open and went back to the kitchen, he'll give Vlad half an hour to study the portion of the battery charger he could see above the tub's rim.

First the airline ticket, Air France, Paris-Chicago-Paris first class, Vladimir Tarasov, open return, purchased the day before the flight. Vlad's passport was from the Republic of Serbia, showed Vlad to be born in Sarajevo on 23 November 1981, his address as Kneza Milosa 15 in Belgrade. John made notes on a yellow pad and listed the dates and places of Vlad's trips using the dates shown in the stamps on his passport, that were not many. Vlad's prior trip to the U.S. was in July of this year, entered at Chicago of the fifth and departed from Chicago on the twenty-second. Two things were clear from the dates in Vlad's passport. First, Vlad was not in the United States at the time of Jack's death. Second, Vlad had left Europe in a hurry since he bought his ticket just before he left.

Vlad's Blackberry was a trove of information. Since arriving in Chicago Vlad had made four international calls and three calls to a number to Muskegon, Michigan. There were also calls to numbers in the Chicago area. John called the international operator to decipher the codes; there of the international calls were to Marseille, France, the other call was made to Sarajevo. The

Muskegon number was The Sportsman Home, Anton's shop. The Chicago calls were to the Airport Marriott and to a car rental agency.

The Blackberry's address book listed twenty-nine names, each with at least one telephone number, several with more than one, all but four of the numbers in Marseille. The number Vlad had called three times was one of two numbers listed under 'Novak'. There was no listing for Stephen, Bobby or Vesic. It had taken John nearly two hours to collect and organize the data, it was now ten minutes past eight; John checked that Vlad was secure and walked two blocks to bring the Cadillac to his driveway.

Vlad had his eyes fixed on the battery charger. John peeled off the duct tape that covered Vlad's mouth and this started breathing heavily through his mouth. "My name is John. What's your name?"

— "My name is 'Fuck you.'"

— "Open your mouth."

— "Fuck you."

— "Are you repeating your name or are you insulting me?" John took the Taser X26C from the vanity and gave Vlad a ten-second jolt, opened Vlad's mouth and stuck one of the two short pieces of wood he had cut out from an old broom and used duct tape to secure the wood piece. Vlad woke up.

— "Now listen good, Mr. You, I'm going to give you the rules of this game. First rule, I am in charge and you are not. Second rule, you must answer my questions and silence is considered to be a wrong answer. Third rule, when your answer is wrong you'll get zapped. You got that? I'm sure you did. You should, you're Novak's best boy." Vlad's eyes opened wider when he heard 'Novak'. "So far I've zapped you with the stun gun, that's not so hard to take. From now on, you'll get zapped with this contraption, the red one in front of your face, this is serious zapping. I'm going to give you a three-second sample, after that each zap will be thirty seconds, at your end of the wires that feels like a whole month. And it won't kill you, I can zap you all night every twenty minutes and you won't die. You'll wish you'll die but you won't." John made sure the terminals were firm on the chains, turned the battery charger to 'On' and rotated the handle clockwise to give Vlad a three-second jolt. Vlad's body jumped up and down and his head hit the tub sides making his nose bleed more. John cut the current off and went to work on the Blackberry for thirty minutes.

— "That was a three-second zap Mr. You, make an effort to imagine what thirty seconds will be like. I know about this stuff, trust me you'll talk, the best guys I've seen can take five zappings, never seen anybody go to six, five is the record, Why take four more?" John removed the duct tape and the wood stick, it had Vlad's teeth's mark on it. "Now, about your name, I don't want to call you by your last name, Mr. You, it's too formal, and your first name is offensive, so I will call you Vladimir, that's a nice name, it has a good ring to it." Vlad was recovering, his color was back and his breathing was better.

— "I was … told …you don't … torture in America." It was difficult for Vlad to talk.

— "We make exceptions for guys like you." We Americans don't believe it's right for people to march into other people's countries and start killing the locals, not only it is illegal but it is bad manners too." John disconnected the terminals from the chains. "And what I'm doing to you is not torture, it's an enhanced interrogation technique."

— "You better kill me now, I'm not going to tell you anything, I'm a patriot."

— "That answer is puzzling to me Vladimir, you have a Serbian passport but you were born in Sarajevo which is in Bosnia, your address is in Belgrade and you live in France. You're a patriot of which country? Remember rules two and three, you've got to answer."

— "I'm a Serb, I'm a Serbian patriot."

— "Good Vladimir, now you're cooperating, we'll be done with this part soon, I have one main question and two or three little questions. Tell me Vladimir, where can I find Stephen Vesic?"

— "Vesic's in hell, I sent him there." So Vesic was dead.

— "Then Vesic was not a patriot like you."

— "Vesic was corrupt."

— "Who's Novak?

— "He's my uncle." John reached for the terminals and Vlad screamed. "He's my uncle, he's my boss too."

— "And why does Novak want me dead?"

— "I don't know." John used the stun gun before he placed the wood stick and the tape on Vlad's mouth and waited for Vlad to wake up to connect the terminals and give him a three-second zap. Vlad convulsed and cried, John removed the tape and the stick. "Please kill me." John left and came back with a glass of cold water.

— "I will not kill you Vladimir, I give you my word on that. Don't know was not a good answer, it did get you zapped. Again, Why did Novak send you to kill me?" Vlad started to cry hard and John realized Vlad did not know. "You know what day is tomorrow Vladimir?"

— "Is eleven or twelve December, something like that."

— "Wrong answer but it will not get you zapped. Tomorrow is the day you will regret you've been born, mark my words on that. Did Vesic kill my son?"

— "I don't know. Please don't hurt me more, I don't know. I don't think so, Vesic did not have the skill."

— "You telephoned Sarajevo, Did you call Mama? Or was it Papa Tarasov? I'm going to fly there and I will kill them both and then I'll go to Marseille and I'll kill your Uncle Novak."

— "That will be the day."

— "So Uncle Novak is a tough guy? Interesting. Question, Who else did Novak send you to kill?" This time Vlad did not hesitate.

— "Somebody who owns a boat, somebody called Monty." That was the answer John was expecting, the picture was getting clearer.

Dealing with the vehicles was time consuming. First John had to bring the SUV inside and drag Vlad from the bath tub to the garage. Lifting Vlad onto the SUV was hard work. The two lengths of chain went into the SUV too. Next John drove the Porsche to the curb to make room in the garage for the Cadillac and finally John moved the battery charger and the cables back to the garage, a great deal of work and he was only half done.

John drove the SUV south on Route 17 and then south on Route 92 until he found the entrance to the dirt road that leads to the wild area between Cypress Lake and Lake Kissimmee. He swung the gate open and closed it back behind the SUV and drove fourteen miles to arrive at a gate closed with a heavy chain hanging at waist height between two hefty wood posts; the padlock resisted the bolt cutter but finally gave up. John crossed over to lift the chain and used a wire to tie its end to the post and hung the lock from the chain so if a Park guard were to drive by he would not notice that the lock had been broken. He searched the top of the dike with his flashlight, nothing there, John did not need a snake bite. The vegetation around the pond's edge was thick grass high enough to hide the SUV; there are few trees in this section of the park where ducks stop every winter on their way to the warmth of South America. Seven years had passed since John had brought Kopernik to the dike and not much had changed. The dike was no more than four or five feet above the water level and at the bottom of its slope the mud reflected the moon light and had the appearance of a silver mirror. It was very quiet, only the breeze caressing the top of the tall grasses, and not a light anywhere to be seen. John pulled the box from the back seat and tossed chicken parts and meat pieces as far as he could, into the pond. Soon there were sounds, subtle sounds of thick skin sliding on mud and the sound of water ripples reaching the mud flats. John pulled the duct tape from Vlad's mouth and rolled him out of the SUV. Vlad hit the ground with his back and John rolled him to the edge of the road. Vlad could see the dirt slope and the mud at the bottom and the water; he started crying and spoke in a language John did not understand.

— "You people killed my son and my son's friend, you pay for them Vladimir. You're the first installment."

— "You said you would not kill me."

— "I'm not going to kill you, I'm recycling you, you're coming back as alligator shit."

John used his right foot to push Vlad over the edge and Vlad rolled down the slope and came to rest on the mud flat at the water's edge. The sound of skin rubbing the mud intensified, John saw the moonlight reflecting on the ripples and heard the hissing noise gators make when they are excited. The gators were asserting themselves and it would be the most aggressive male that soon will grab the white body and drag it down to the depths of the pond.

John had difficulty turning the SUV around and when he backed to the top of the dike and he looked out the white body was not there.

CHAPTER 12
PIESECKI

IT WAS SIX O'CLOCK on Tuesday morning when John turned onto Route 17 North, realized he did not have the energy to drive home and stopped at a hotel near one of Disney's Parks. At three in the afternoon John woke up feeling cold, he had set the air conditioning too low. He burned Vlad's photograph and let the ashes fall in the toilette. The call to Gianni DiRenzo was short, he arranged to meet Gianni's men at a bar near Jack's house on Thursday evening. He showered and shaved before he called Carol and stayed on the phone for longer than an hour. John ate in his room, watched a basketball game on television and went back to bed at nine to have a second good night sleep. John was up at six.

Before returning the SUV to the rental agency at Orlando International Airport John took it to a car wash to have the interior vacuumed and the exterior washed twice. He rode a cab back to Paradise Gardens, cleaned the tub and tidied up the house. He was ready for the phone call. John had distributed the contents of Jack's manila envelope on the dining table.

— "Mr. Ben Piesecki please, this is John O'Rourke, Mr. Piesecki is expecting my call."

It did not take long. "I'm sorry I did not call you Monday morning as I said I would but I found my mail for the last two weeks and there was a fat envelope from Jack. I wanted to digest the contents before we spoke. Did you have a chance to find Vesic's address?"

— "I did, Buckingham Import-Export, 229 Sabine Street," It was the address John already had.

— "I've been there, it's a dead end." John remained silent waiting for Piesecki to ask the obvious question.

— "You said you received documents from Jack. Anything that may interest me?" John remained silent. "I mean are these documents related to my firm?" Piesecki's voice was strained; John did not answer. "Did you look at them? Maybe you can bring them over my office, we'll talk." No answer from John, three or four seconds went by. "It'll be beneficial to all of us if we keep matters confidential, all of us will benefit. If you don't want to meet here I'll be happy to come see you." Piesecki had shown his hand.

— "I didn't say documents, I said contents, there is more than just documents. And they have to do with your firm, and with you Piesecki, with you personally. And for mc to deliver this stuff to you it'll have to be very beneficial, I want a three with six zeroes in front, that sort of beneficial. Otherwise I'll go straight to Mr. Taylor."

— "I don't have access to that much, there will have to be some negotiation, if we could meet later maybe."

— "I want cash in two days, Friday night, we'll make the exchange when you have the cash. And you'll have to give me Vesic too, without Vesic there is no deal."

— "I'll have to call you back. Let me have a number where I can reach you."

John spent half an hour returning everything to its place in the garage. He put part of Vlad's cash in his pant's pockets and placed the rest of it and Vlad's Glock in the tool box where he had kept Vlad's other pistol and returned the tool box back to its place under the work bench. He filled two garbage bags with the refrigerator contents, John was not planning to be back very soon. One hour had gone by and Pisecki had not called back; not scared enough or maybe too scared. John called the same number. "No, Mr. Piesecki had to leave for a meeting, we don't expect Mr. Piesecki to be back until tomorrow." Like hell he will.

— "May I speak to Mr. Taylor's secretary please?"

Mrs. Ward was very cordial. "Let me see if Mr. Taylor is available. Tell me your name again please." It took only twenty seconds.

— "Mr. O'Rourke, how are you?" John had expected Mr. Taylor to be friendly and he was.

— "Let me cut to the chase. On Monday I returned to my house in Orlando and I found my mail for the last two weeks and there was an envelope from my son, dated the day he died. It has to do with what has been taken from your company. I thought you may want to resolve this matter before the Army auditors arrive in January. From what I read it seems that your man Piesecki has a lot to do with your losses."

— "Of course I want to resolve this matter, the Army expects us to run a very tight ship and does not tolerate irregularities, not that they should. So you are in Florida then? Lucky you, it's thirty degrees in Chicago. And how do you propose to resolve this matter, as you put it so well? What is your proposition?"

— "I'm a simple man, Mr. Taylor, I have what you need and you have what I want. I'll help you avoid problems with the Army auditors and you'll help me improve the rest of my life. What I want from you is peanuts for a man of your position."

— "And if I don't."

— "Then I'll do what my son asked me to do."

— "We don't need to resort to that, we'll find an accommodation such that we will both profit, I will deal with Piesecki later as a separate matter. And when, how and where do you propose to complete our transaction?"

— "This is the deal, three million dollars in cash, two days from today. I'll give you what Jack sent to me. I'll come to your house on the waterfront and I want to see your daughter Julie there to make sure nothing funny happens. Friday night, ten o'clock, your house, I know where it is. I'll have friends drive me in, they'll come back for me when I'm ready, I don't want to take chances carrying all that money." Mr. Taylor got John's message.

— "We have agreed on a deal then. I'm perfectly happy with your terms, losing my contracts would be more costly and would put a lot of my people out of work. We don't want that, Do we? Of course not."

— "Then it's Friday night at ten, your house." John hung up, soon he'd be a rich man, he had managed to transform adversity into a success. Three mil from Taylor, one-and-a-half mil from Adamson plus Vlad's allowance. John served himself a glass of cold milk and sat at the table to look at the contents of the envelope Jack had mailed from Chicago three weeks earlier, a dozen photographs of Tricia and her two children, and wondered when and if he'll be seeing Tricia and his grandchildren again.

John drove Vlad's Cadillac to the long-term parking at the airport, ate lunch before boarding and arrived at Denver International Airport in the late afternoon. He rented a Lincoln with a V-eight engine and drove to Golden for his items. It did not take long for Terry to show how to screw the bottle, adjust the oxygen and set the timer; John spent the night at the McKenna's and was on his way to Chicago ten minutes after four on Thursday morning, He had one tin box sealed with duct tape secured between the passenger seat and the rear seat with his black overcoat on top of it, the other tin box in the Lincoln's trunk propped with his luggage. The Colt forty-five and the clips he borrowed from Terry were in the glove compartment.

It took John sixteen hours to drive the thousand miles to Chicago, he made only two quick stops and spoke to Carol several times along the way. Pauley was waiting at Dooley's Bar with the four men from San Diego and did not complain that John was two hours late. They had drinks and light food at Dooley's before they drove to Jack's house; in and out in fifteen minutes, John carried the posters wrapped in a red blanket tied with a white cord he took from a pair of pajama's pants. One of the Gualdieri brothers took John to spend the night at his house and cooked frittata with spicy chorizo for breakfast. At ten John visited with Gene Kazmierski at his office to see if there were new developments, there were none, the consensus was that Jack's assassin was a professional and that they may solve the case only with a tip. Motives were not addressed.

— "Gene, did you check Jack's brother's whereabouts the night of the killings? And DeSimone's?"

Captain Kazmierski did not need to consult the files. "DeSimone went to play bridge at a private club; a dozen men vouched for him. He arrived at the club before seven and stayed until past midnight, was there all the time. Sean and Sarah Adamson had tickets for a subscription concert but did not show up; they lied to us that they were at the concert. We have their seats numbers and checked with those in the adjacent seats, they were not at the concert. We're following that up, except that Sean Adamson is in Europe and not expected back until next week. I have a tail on his wife. What about you?"

— "I've been following the Vlasic's trail and did not get anywhere. I'm out of ideas."

— "Take a break. Go somewhere with Mackenzie, take her to Florida."

— "I'll take you up on that. Will you give Carol time off, say two, three weeks, we'll go on a vacation."

— "Two weeks with pay, two more weeks if she wants them. How's that?"

— "Deal, four weeks, I'll talk to Carol later today."

— "Marry the woman, that's what she wants."

Monty had not returned John's call and it was close to seven, so John called and Monty said he was working on the boat and had been distracted with all that was going on around him. "Monty, if your offer is still up I'll take advantage and I'll stay on your boat, two nights, tonight and tomorrow night, I'll be leaving for San Diego and Hawaii on Monday, I have a date, How about that? May I come over?"

— "Sure, I'll be here, always in the boat on Friday nights. Come early, we'll eat at the restaurant."

— "So long as they close very late. I won't make it to the boat until around ten or eleven."

— "I'll have food sent over or we'll order pizza, I've got plenty of beer. I'll see you tonight then. Listen, we had a big commotion here earlier today. Immigration officers went over Mr. Taylor's yacht and pulled the captain and the two crew to the Club office, it happens that one of the crew is a Spaniard without proper documents and the Immigration people were taking about putting him on a plane to Mexico and the agents called the Spanish Consulate and the Consul drove over and it's like a soap opera here, now they're waiting for Julie Taylor to arrive and bail the guy out. Thirty thousand dollar bond, I guess for the Taylor's is pocket change. Tonight I'll give you the rest of the story."

Carol met John at seven fifteen at the McDonald's parking lot, John exchanged Terry O'Leary's forty-five for his own weapon and magazines and left in Pauley's car when the chronometer John kept hanging from his neck showed six hours and thirty minutes to go. The show was on. Three cars pulled from the lot and followed Pauley's until two blocks before John's destination and then stayed behind. The four cars had on their roofs the kind of red, white and blue lights police cars and emergency vehicles have, two sets each car. Pauley answered John's question while he fiddled with the radio volume. "We rent them, they're legal, just that you're not supposed to turn them on. We've done worst before. Johnny, you should come work with us, you're more like us than like your buddies. Mister DiRenzo likes you." Pauley turned the radio off. "Now tell me again about the call."

— "I'll ring you, you say hello, I say 'John' and I hang up. You wait exactly five minutes and turn all the lights on and leave them on until I call again. You'll know it's me, you'll see it's my number, won't talk to you."

— "Can't keep the lights on for too long. Your buddies will show up and we'll be in trouble."

— "You'll have to figure that one out by yourself. It won't be more than five, six minutes, all I need is to make an impression. After that, send the cars away and pull off your lights before you come back for me. Are we on the same page?"

— "Yeah, we'll be alright. Good luck, Johnny." They had arrived at possibly the most elegant of all of Chicago's high-rise condominium buildings, thirty-six stories, underground garage, helicopter pad. A red Ferrari and a silvery blue Aston Martin were parked in between fat columns and a stretch limousine was waiting at the curb closest to the building with its rear doors facing the building fully open. Two young men dressed in valet uniforms were standing next to the limo and a third one approached Pauley's car, but Pauley drove off before the young man reached the driver's window. Enrico Gualdieri was walking up the ramp to join John, who waited for Enrico to arrive and pointed up to several spots overhead. "I counted four cameras outside. There will be plenty more inside the lobby. Keep your eyes level, don't look at the floor and don't take your hat off." John checked his wrist watch, ten minutes to eight. They approached the concierge's desk, one man was sitting down watching a bank of television monitors, the other smiled to John.

— "Good evening. Are you expected?" The concierge glanced at the manila envelope John was carrying, it looked empty.

John pulled and opened his wallet to show his badge. "I'm Lieutenant O'Rourke of the Chicago Police Department, this is Sergeant D'Arienzo. We're expected at the Taylor residence."

— "Mr. and Mrs. Taylor or Miss Taylor?"

— "Mister Taylor, he's expecting me. But before you call, help me out. How many surveillance cameras?"

— "Can't tell you that, you'll have to go through channels. I work for the security company, could loose my job. Call my office after eight Monday morning, the bosses will be there, they'll take care of you."

— "It's all right. I take it you watch the monitors full time and you keep the tapes. That so?"

— "I can tell you that. Yes, and we change tapes noon and midnight, we store them. The building is very conscious of liability claims, many important people here. You go through my office Lieutenant, talk to the bosses and I'll show you the entire set-up."

— "Tell me if you can help me with this. Mr. Taylor wants to see the kind of tape you use, an empty tape. Do you think you'll be able to take a minute later on and come upstairs and show Mr. Taylor the kind of tape you use. I just want to make a point. Can you help me out? I'll tear two of your parking tickets in return, Deal?"

— "That sounds like a deal."

— "Good, write your name and the phone number at the desk, I'll ring you when Mr. Taylor is ready. Now you may call Mr. Taylor."

It took a while, Mr. Taylor said to wait. John made two full turns on his feet to see the extent of the lobby. Not much furniture but very elegant, every piece seemed to be of a scale larger than normal. On the far left side of the lobby a marble fireplace, a real fireplace with wood logs burning strong, a group of chairs and a sofa in front of the fireplace, one man reading a newspaper. A large round table with a pink marble top half way between the concierge's desk and the entrance. A bank of four elevators to one side, two elevators on the opposite side. Lamps, more chairs, a black grand piano with a chandelier on top. Liberace was missing. Two ladies in long evening dresses and dark coats standing up near the entrance, probably waiting for somebody else to come before walking to the limousine waiting outside.

Mr. Taylor called the concierge back in twelve minutes. John and Enrico never moved away from the desk any remained silent. "Mr. Taylor said to come up, I need to go with you. We'll use the penthouse elevators." They walked to the pair of elevator on the right side, Mark the Concierge ran a plastic card through a slot, the doors slid open and the three walked inside the car, all cherry wood and mirrors, two small cameras at opposite corners. There were five buttons marked G, L, 34, 35 and 36. John must have made a face because Mark volunteered an explanation. "This car goes only to the Taylor's, the thirty-four floor is Ms. Julie Taylor's and the thirty-fifth and thirty-sixth are Mr. and Mrs. Taylor's, they occupy two full floors. The nicest people in the world."

The elevator was very fast, the doors slid open at the thirty-sixth floor, Mark said 'There you go sir, ring me when Mr. Taylor is ready' and John and Enrico stepped out into the ante-chamber to the largest space one would expect in a residence, the ceiling was very high. A thin woman in her fifties dressed in black said "Follow me, Mister Taylor is in his study", not 'the' study, but 'his' study. It was a long walk through a space that looked like what John imagined European palaces to be or maybe like the better palaces in Hollywood films. Windows everywhere, overlooking Lake Michigan. The lady knocked at the door before opening it and Mr. Taylor walked out dressed in gray flannel pants and a navy blue V-neck over a white shirt.

— "You said you'll be here at ten, it's only eight, my daughter is not here yet." Mr. Taylor looked at Enrico Gualtieri for an instant and then back at John. "You did not mention a companion."

— "Sergeant D'Arienzo is here so I feel comfortable. I came earlier because I had no choice, I'll explain after we finish our transaction." Mr. Taylor glanced at the empty-looking manila envelope John held in his left hand.

— "You did not bring what I'm supposed to get."

— "I did, it's here." Mr. Taylor turned on his heels and walked into his studio; it was rather dark with one bright light coming from a lamp sitting on a desk; several books that looked to John like photograph albums were spread open on the desk. The desk faced the door they entered on, one chair with a tall back behind the desk, one chair in front. On the wall behind the desk a large painting depicting a city scape in the rain, mostly grays and browns; a set of French doors with the drapes drawn, leading to a balcony, tall bookcases lined against the walls. There was a small door on one of the side walls, John guessed a bathroom. Two gilded chairs and a gilded love seat upholstered in a silvery fabric with thin red lines, a Persian rug underneath. A very elegant room. No photographs, no bar. John walked towards the gilded chairs, took his overcoat off and laid it on the love seat.

— "I was working on my stamps. Please come sit down." Mr. Taylor motioned to the chair in front of his desk and walked around to the chair behind. "I'm afraid those chairs are meant to look at not to sit on, they're Early Empire, nearly two hundred years old, a bit fragile and very valuable, I have lent them to Museums." Mr. Taylor smiled a condescending smile.

— "At the end of the day you will find out these chairs to be totally irrelevant. I'm comfortable here, we can see each other." There was no coffee table so John laid the manila envelope on his legs. "We have a lot to talk and not much time."

— "You do not have what I need."

— "In the envelope, one sheet of paper and a computer disk. John sent a note too but I'm keeping that." John opened the envelope and pulled a square plastic container with one computer disk inside and a photocopy of the spreadsheet Jack had left folded in John Grisham's book. John held both high and Mr. Taylor left the security of his desk and walked to the gilded chair in front of John. "There are hundreds of pages in the disk, photocopies of documents and spreadsheets, I looked at them all and got the gist of your situation. The sheet of paper is in the disk too, it's the summary. Look at the date on the top right corner, the Friday before Jack's death; the fourth column has the weights, look at the bottom, twelve thousand plus kilos. You may look at the disk later." John handed the sheet of paper and the plastic container to Mr. Taylor.

— "How do I know you did not make copies?"

— "I made two copies and Monday afternoon I will deliver them to a Law firm and to a Bank for safekeeping in case something sudden happens to me. I'm sure you understand. At any rate, once you go through your audit, the disk and the paper lose their importance." I'm confident that your man Piesecki is already making the necessary corrections using what Jack discovered." Mr. Taylor was thinking about 'Monday afternoon', that is two and a half days for Novak's nephew to carry out his work.

— "You received these in Orlando? You where there then?"

— "Only on Monday morning, at noon I drove to Winter Park to play golf and stayed there with friends until I flew back." That would explain why Novak's nephew had not carried out his work.

— "Well, you're here now. What is that the reason you came early?"

— "After we're done with our transaction. You have what I promised, I want what's coming to me."

'What's coming to you, you will get over the weekend, just wait for Novak's boy to find you' was Mr. Taylor's thought. "I have a valise behind my desk, I'll get it." As Mr. Taylor walked to his desk John stood up and grabbed the semiautomatic in his pants's right pocket, but did not pull it out. It did not go unnoticed to Mr. Taylor, who bent to lift a cast-aluminum briefcase hidden behind the desk. "Three million dollars, thousands and five-hundred notes, you may look at it."

John opened the briefcase and shuffled several stacks of five-hundred and thousand-dollar bills to ascertain they were currency, not cut pieces of paper. "It seems it's all there." John sat the briefcase to the left of his chair. "I guess this is small potatoes to you."

— "The transaction is completed, Why were you early?"

— "I came early because you'll be arrested tonight. Tonight after ten o'clock."

— "Nonsense, Arrested for what?"

— "For the murder of my son and his partner Christian Adamson. You and your man Piesecki. They haven't captured him but they will soon, Piesecki will not be able to disappear."

— "Total nonsense."

— "Nonsense? Where were you the night of the murders? I'm sure you'll remember that."

— "I was here."

— "You were at my son's house. You and Piesecki."

— "I've never been to your son's house. I had no reason to."

— "You're absolutely sure? Think about it, I don't want you to tell me five minutes from now that you forgot about that one time …"

— "I'm absolutely sure, I was here that night and every night of that week, and every other night except for the night of the party at my company. My wife is very ill, I spend most of my time with her and certainly every evening. Every evening." Mr. Taylor did not lose his composure.

— "So you are absolutely certain?"

— "Positively sure."

— "My colleagues have hair samples taken from the sofa in Jack's house. The sofa across the sofa where Jack and Christian were found. They've been matching hair specimens for two weeks, they matched yours two days ago."

— "My hair has not been sampled, they have nothing to compare with."

— "Yes they do. You're too important a person to ask you for a sample, they had to make sure first so they got the sample from your barber, he was happy to cooperate." Mr. Taylor made a face to show his disdain for the barber.

— "Such is not legal, it carries no weight."

— "Of course it isn't legal, the Captain ordered that just to make sure. The Captain will get your hair tonight and this time it will be legal. They'll do more than cut your hair, the fabric in Jack's sofas is very fibrous, my people will take every piece of clothing you own and every shoe in this wonderful residence of yours and they'll put it all under the microscope, mark my words, they'll find fibers that match those in Jack's sofa. They'll check every room, they'll check your daughter's flat too, just in case, they obtained all the necessary subpoenas this afternoon. They-will-nail-you."

— "Never mind my hair, I told you I was here, I was in my house at the time your son was killed."

John took his cellular out of his coat pocket and called Mark the Concierge's number. "Mark, Mr. Taylor is ready for you, please bring the tape now." John kept his cell phone in his right hand, found Pauley's number, pressed the 'Send' button and hung up immediately.

It took only a few minutes for Mark to arrive. As John heard the knock on the studio door he pressed the 'Send' button twice to ring Pauley's number and Pauley answered. "John." And hung up. That was the signal for the lights to go on in five minutes. John looked at the time on the telephone screen.

— "There is a man from downstairs to see you." The lady in the black dress entered the room and Mark followed her.

— "Good evening Mr. Taylor." Mr. Taylor recognized Mark from downstairs.

Mark handed the tape cartridge to John. "Thank you Mark. The tapes are changed at noon and midnight, Right?"

— "Right, same time every day Lieutenant. Good night Mr. Taylor."

— "I'll return the tape to you as I leave. My colleagues will be here any time now." Mark nodded and left. "This is a blank tape for you to see." John tossed it towards his overcoat but he missed and the tape cartridge fell to the floor. "There are four cameras in the entrance, outside the building, four cameras in the lobby and two in each elevator. You were recorded every time you came in and every time you left the building, and the dates and times are on the tapes." John stood up and looked at his telephone screen, one minute to go. Mr. Taylor sat deep in his gilded Empire chair. "You practically confessed to me fifteen minutes ago." Mr. Taylor was looking at the floor thinking about the tapes and what they show. "Come with me to the balcony, you'll see the cars, they should be here by now." Mr. Taylor walked to the glass parapet at the edge of the balcony and looked down to see the flashing red, white and blue lights on top of four cars parked beyond the porte-cochere. "My people will secure the building first, elevators, stairs, helicopter pad, then they'll go through the subpoenas and finally they will sequester the tapes. Only after all that they will come for you, it'll be at least two hours before they come get you. There is no way out Taylor, you'll be wearing an orange suit before the sun is up."

Mr. Taylor was confused, not being used to situations where he was not the one in control. He did not want Julie to arrive with all this going on, the incident with Immigration had been fortunate, Was Julie still there? He had to stop her from coming. Mr. Taylor anticipated the embarrassment, he needed time. Mr. Taylor returned to his chair and waited for John to lock the French doors and sit down.

— "I told you before you practically confessed to me as soon as I arrived. You were expecting a hundred sheets of paper as those you took from Jack's briefcase before leaving his house; you were surprised that the envelope was so thin. That was enough for me, not for a court of law, but it was for me." Mr. Taylor was staring at the Persian rug. "I'll tell you how you did it."

— "You must be enjoying this."

— "Immensely. I thought I would feel sorry for an old man like you but I don't."

— "I need to call my daughter, I don't want her to be exposed to all of this. You have a daughter, In Germany, is that right?"

— "That's right."

— "So you speak German?

— "I'm afraid I'm a one-language man."

Mr. Taylor walked towards the French doors to telephone Julie and when Julie answered he turned to face the doors and spoke German. "Don't come here, things are going very wrong for me and I don't want you to be here and be part of it. Leave right now. Be careful where you go and stay away for a while." Tears came down as he listened to his only daughter for several minutes. "I love you, Babushka, and your mother loves you too. I'll detain these people for as long as I can." Mr. Taylor decided to listen to the damn fool for as long as he wished to speak and after that he would take his time to tell his own story, that would help Julie get away and escape all the grief.

— "You were going to tell me?"

— "I'll tell you why you killed my son and how you did it. You and Piesecki thought yourselves very clever but you implicated yourselves in every step you took. You hired Jack's firm to carry out an audit of your operation so you would know if you needed to revise your records before the Army's audit, but it backfired. You underestimated my son's skills. Jack was very thorough and studied the production process of your wonderful SA-286 and compared the weight of the components coming into the plant to the weight of the final product that left the plant and discovered a difference of more than twelve thousand kilos. First Jack thought that somebody was stealing from you by inflating the purchases but near the end Jack realized that was not the case, that it wasn't an excess of components weight, but a shortage in the weight of the final product, and he concluded that twelve thousand kilos of a very powerful explosive compound were out on the street. Jack suspected plant personnel were removing the explosive from the plant, he did not realize it was you and Piesecki stealing from yourselves. What do you get in the open market for twelve thousand kilos at say, twenty thousand dollars a kilo? Is it two hundred and forty million dollars? Ten times what the Army pays, Isn't it? Jack wanted you to notify the Army and you could not tell him not to worry, that it was you and Piesecki removing the explosives. So when you and Piesecki sat with Jack in his office that last Monday you decided that Jack had to be silenced. You stayed behind drinking coffee with DeSimone and told him that Jack had done a fine job and how happy you were, not to be suspected, Right?"

If that is what the fool wanted to believe, let the fool believe it. "Right."

— "We know exactly at what time Piesecki left and at what time you left because we have the tapes from the elevators and from the lobby in Jack's place of work. Piesecki had your driver take him home to get his own car, we know he lives not far from you, and he returned in his car to Jack's office to pick you up. But you don't go around carrying a weapon, you had to come home to retrieve your twenty-two caliber target pistol and a couple of bottles of Champagne and on the way to Jack's you picked up some food."

Mr. Taylor was half listening to John's relation and half considering what he would do next. "So you and Piesecki showed up at Jack's all smiles and said you came in to work things out and you sat down and ate and had a few glasses and you told Jack and Christian that you would take a photograph of them with Piesecki in the middle so Piesecki placed himself behind the sofa and shot them both in the head. You old bastard killed my son and his friend. For what? For more money? How much is enough?"

— "Money has nothing to do with it. Finish your story and I'll tell you mine." Let the fool talk some more, let him believe he's right.

— "Your problem is that you will be placed in this building, coming in and going out, the outside cameras will confirm the car Piesecki drove and unfortunately for you and Piesecki there are three traffic cameras between this building and Jack's house, it'll take time but my people will find the frame with your car and the frame will give them the time, that is enough to show you had the opportunity. You will be nailed and Piesecki will too. Only that Piesecki may turn State witness and point at you as the killer, after all it was your pistol, Wasn't it? It' be at least twenty years in Joliet no matter which part you played. You'll die in prison."

Talk, fool, talk all you want, enjoy the sound of your voice, you won't be talking much when Novak's boy finds you next Monday. "It was my pistol."

— "You took the documents from Jack's briefcase. You had seen Jack from Monty DeSimone's office as he was leaving carrying a fat briefcase. And after you killed Jack, you took everything from Jack's briefcase, except that Jack had made copies that he mailed to me on his way home, that's what's in the disk I gave you. You also took with you the trash bag from the kitchen with everything you and Piesecki had brought to Jack's house, and the bag from the paper shredder too. What you left behind was your hair on the back of Jack's sofa."

The fool had no more to say. "Money has nothing to do with it, I did what I did for the fatherland."

— "The fatherland? You lived all your life in this country, You call yourself a German? You were a child when your father brought you to America. Is that how you show your gratitude?"

— "You said your part, now it's my turn, I'll tell you my story and my father's story too." And I will take my time, you fool. "I was not born in Berlin, my father took my mother to Belgrade for me to be born there. We are Serbs and my father was a patriot. He wanted me to be born in Serbia. My father was sent to Moscow in nineteen twenty to establish contact with the new regime. Before that time, my father had prepared explosives for our freedom fighters, the Black Hand, for many years. You see, my father knew Gavrilo Princip." John's expression revealed that the name did not register. "Princip shot Archduke Ferdinand in Sarajevo and started the Great War. Twenty-eight June nineteen eighteen. The Black Hand worked for the emancipation of Serbia and to join with the Serbs in Bosnia. We're still fighting for it. Only that it is not convenient for the great powers. The explosives are for my comrades to use in the liberation of Serbia."

— "Your father was first a communist and then a Nazi."

— "My father was neither. My father accomplished what he had to do in Russia, but he joined the losing faction and had to escape when Leon Trotski left. He stayed in Germany because he was told to establish contact with the Nazi's. And when the Nazi's lost the war my father had no choices, the military brought him to America to exploit his talent, so he came here and continued serving the Fatherland. I do the same. Your son's death was an unfortunate accident, your son gave us no choices. It had nothing to do with money, it had to do with supplying my comrades."

— "And Vesic?"

— "Vesic was a trivial part of our operation. Vesic arranged for certain shipments. Your son found the record of one payment my company made to Vesic and one bill of lading from five or six years ago. A totally forgotten item. Your son's death is very unfortunate but these things happen, the military call it collateral damage. Believe what you want but I'm sorry about your son."

— "I know how you removed the explosives from the factory. You took the samples brought to the laboratory for testing, a few kilos from each of three shifts, every day, it adds up. It was stored in your office and you and Piesecki carried it to your helicopter when you left the plant. Nobody screens the boss, Right?" Mr. Taylor showed no reaction, his face was like a mask, very pale. "Your wife ran the testing laboratory, Didn't she?"

Let the fool believe what he wishes to be believe. "My wife is a Serbian patriot too." It was now time to ask the question. "What will it take to stop your people to come over for me? I can pay you five times what you have, I have funds in Europe. You may ask for whatever you want."

— "It can't be done, you have no way out of this building. The only thing that will stop my people is a heart attack or something of that sort, can't prosecute a dead man. No other way, you're short of choices."

— "It's time for you to leave." John stood up to put on his overcoat and walked to the door with the aluminum briefcase in his left hand.

— "Will you leave your pistol with me?" John neither answered nor did he turn around.

CHAPTER 13
SATISFACTION

JOHN ALTERNATED FACING EACH of the cameras in the elevator and then looked straight at two of them in the lobby. Enrico kept his hat on and his eyes level. "What time do you have Mark?" John looked at his wrist watch. "You sure, check it out." John checked his wrist watch for the second time. "So ten twenty it is, make sure you log me out." John wanted his departure time to be well documented. Pauley was waiting across the street and drove to the porte-cochere as soon as he saw John and Enrico leaving the lobby.

— "Will Gianni be there?" John had placed the aluminum briefcase between his legs and his seat.

— "Yes, Mister DiRenzo is already waiting for us in the Yacht Club parking lot. The guard never saw it coming, my guys are keeping him gagged in one of the cars, he ain't going nowhere. We'll be at the Yacht Club inside twenty minutes."

— "What will you do with the guard?"

— "What do you mean Johnny? You think we're gonna kill the poor guy? When we're done we'll give the guy ten grand to keep for himself and we'll warn him if he says one word to anybody we come back and get him. What do you think we are? Gangsters?"

Pauley drove into the Yacht Club's parking lot and dropped off John at his car. John left the aluminum briefcase and his top coat in the trunk and joined Gianni, who was leaning on a heavy cane and had the two wrestler-size gorillas flanking him. The four walked slowly to Monty's boat as Gianni was not totally used to his new hips as yet.

— "It would help if you loose some weight Gianni."

— "Right, winning the Lotto would help me too." They stopped twice along the way for Gianni to rest his legs. One of the gorillas was carrying a box, the other a bottle in each hand. "I've been waiting for this moment, John." Gianni hit the wood deck twice with his right foot as if he were a horse reading for a race. "You sure the radio's gonna work?"

— "It should work, if it doesn't there is not much we can do. We'll have to see. Let me go first." John boarded the sail boat and went inside the cabin. Monty was wearing white shorts and a gray sweat shirt with 'Bulls' in red block letters and was reading a paperback. No shoes. "Monty, I took the liberty of bringing a friend with me. We are here to use your satellite radio."

— "Do I have a choice? What for?"

— "I have to talk to Julie Taylor?"

— "How do you know they sailed?"

— "I have my ways. At what time did they sail?"

— "Two hours ago, give or take. It took them a while to leave the harbor."

— "So they'd be what? Twenty, thirty miles away?"

— "That boat can do fifteen knots but the Captain won't be pushing her at such speed. All they're doing is testing the engines, so they don't have surprises with the guests on board. They'll be back in a few hours."

— "Then how far are they?"

— "I'd say, hour and a half, ten knots, fifteen miles away." Monty was wrong, Julie was sailing at her cruising speed of fifteen knots, the vessel was twenty two miles away, going north and east.

— "It's twelve twenty now, we'll call Julie at one forty. They'll be where by then?"

— "Another ten miles, but they don't go straight out, they'll be going on a circle, they'll be back before sunlight. I have pizza and empanadas, Ever have those? I have twelve, half meat, half cheese."

— "Let me go get my friend." I was difficult for Gianni DiRenzo to get on board and John had to hold Gianni's left hand for him to keep his balance. The gorillas boarded one at a time and when both were on board the boat leaned to starboard. John entered the cabin first and Gianni followed and turned around to receive the box from Gorilla Number One. "Wait, I have two bottles too." Gorilla Number Two handed the bottles to Gianni. Both large men stayed on the deck.

— o —

The first note Taylor wrote was for his daughter Julie and contained two sentences only. The second note was short too, Taylor confessed to be the one who killed the two men and named Piesecki as his accomplice, gave no reasons and expressed no remorse. He left both notes on his desk under a paper weight.

— "I will be sitting with Mrs. Taylor now, you may take your dinner break, please return in two hours." Nurse Olga stood up and left the chair next to the bed for Mr. Taylor to sit down. Every night the poor man watched his wife rest, exchanging a few words every time Mrs. Taylor woke up. But this was Nurse Olga's job, all her patients were terminal and she had witnessed so much suffering in her twenty years of nursing that by now she was immune to it. "Before you leave please re-charge the morphine pump, Mrs. Taylor may wake up and I don't wish to call you." Mr. Taylor sounded testy, that was so unlike Mr. Taylor. Nurse Olga used the key she had hanging from her neck to turn the morphine pump to zero. "That should be sufficient to keep Mrs. Taylor comfortable for now." And Nurse Olga left happy that she could sit down for her dinner in the kitchen instead of eating off a tray, and maybe watch television for an hour or two. Her shift had started at six in the evening and she had to go until six in the morning.

Mr. Taylor locked the door behind Nurse Olga. He had no time to wait for Catherine to wake up, although he wished a few words with her. He pumped morphine until the beeper sounded twice and sat at the chair to wait for the effect to take place. Mr. Taylor used one of the pillows with the embroidered silk case and cried as he maintained the pressure on his wife's face. It did not take long.

Mr. Taylor's thoughts were about his Little Babushka as he walked to the balcony. The parapet was too high for him to climb and he dragged one of the gilded chairs so he could step over the rail. The fool was right, at the end of the day the gilded chairs had become irrelevant.

— o —

— "Monty, meet my friend Gianni DiRenzo, he's here to listen when I talk to Julie. Gianni's sister is Christian's mother." John moved to his left. "Gianni, this is Monty DeSimone, he was Jack's boss." Gianni had to switch his cane to his left hand to shake hands with Monty.

— "I was more than Jack's boss, I was Jack's friend; and Christian's too. I knew Christian for many years, we paired to play bridge many times. I believe I've met you Mister DiRenzo, years ago."

— "I remember you too. You're Christian's good and trusted friend. Italians like you and me value that. I have a deal to make with you." Gianni opened the box he brought and pulled several plastic containers with sushi, rolls and other foods. "You and Johnny eat this raw fish here and stick to the white wine, my two buddies and me will have your pizza and the Chianti. Deal?"

— "You've got a deal Mr. DiRenzo."

— "Call me Gianni, Christian's friends are my friends." Gorilla Number 1 stepped in and tapped DiRenzo's shoulder; and bent to whisper in DiRenzo's ear. "No need to whisper, we're among friends here." Gorilla Number One had an expression of fear in his face. "Go ahead, it's all right."

— "The man Taylor is dead, he jumped from the top of his building. It's on the radio, Pauley called for me to tell you. Killed his wife before he jumped."

— "Shit Johhny, What did you say to that guy?"

— "I shamed him, that's all I did." John served wine in five glasses. Monty showed no reaction. "Tell your guys to come in, they'll freeze outside." Two electric heaters kept the cabin warm.

— "Where do you get the power?"

— "Everything on the boat is connected to a feed on the dock. What's this about Mr. Taylor?" The two big men came in and suddenly the cabin looked half as large as before.

— "I visited with Taylor earlier today and told him he was going to be arrested for Jack's and Christian's murders and Taylor chose to take the easy way out. I told Taylor that the detectives had found hair on one of Jack's sofas that matched his hair, and I also told Taylor that the security tapes in his building showed him arriving to his building in the evening just before Jack's and

Christian's deaths, and showed him leaving shortly after and coming back later, all at times that coincided with Jack's and Christian's time of death. There is more, but that's the core of it." John ate the last bit of his cheese empanada. "Taylor killed his wife first and then himself to take the blame. I told Taylor a dead man can not be prosecuted. Taylor wanted to protect his accomplice. Was Piesecki around here today by chance?" Monty shook his head. There was no Chianti left. "I'll give Julie the news." John checked his watch. "It's about the right time, show me how to use the radio. Better yet, you call and get Julie on the phone, I'll take it from there."

— "Identify yourself." A voice with a heavy accent answered Monty's call."

— "Please get Miss Julie Taylor."

— "And you are?"

— "Monty DeSimone, Miss Taylor knows who I am." It did not take long.

— "Monty, Surprise!"

— "It's not Monty, it's John O'Rourke."

— "Johnny, Where've you been? We've got to get together." Julie had not been listening to the radio. "You ran away from me."

— "Florida. Where are you going?"

— "You know where I'm going Johnny, no need to beat around the bush, you were with my Dad, my Dad told me everything. Remember? I'm on my way to Muskegon, I'll be meeting Vesic and Anton there. Remember them?" This was not the Julie from days before, her warmth had turned into pure cynicism.

— "Piesecki with you?"

— "He was, but not any longer."

— "Listen good Julie. Vesic's dead, Vlad killed him. And so you know, Vlad will not be waiting for you in Michigan, nor will he be visiting with me any time soon. By now Vlad has become part of the environment. Anton I'll kill just for sport, soon, and Novak I have not made up my mind yet. And you're not sailing for Muskegon, Honey, maybe Milwaukee, maybe Green Bay, more likely some small harbor in Michigan, there are so many of them, but for sure you're not going to Muskegon. I heard your father telling you, I know enough German." John waited for an answer or a comment, none came, his statements had taken the wind from Julie's sails. "I know everything Honey, everything,

125

including how you moved your precious SA-286 out of the factory, very ingenious and very daring." John paused.

— "Simplicity and audacity win battles, Napoleon said it, Or maybe it was General Patton? Can't remember. It was my Mom's idea. What is it to you? Come work for us, my Dad can use someone with your talents, and I like you. What's wrong with that Johnny O'Rourke? Tell me how you think we did it." Julie was probing. Smart.

— "Two parties every year, all security personnel amusing themselves inside the tent, big trucks removing the remains of the party and in the process picking up the boxes stored in your father's and mother's sanctuary, twelve thousand kilos of explosives moved in clear view over five years. And how did your father get ahold of the explosive? From the laboratory, the specimens to be tested that were not, ten, fifteen kilos per shift, three shifts per day, in six months it adds up to tons. And how were the specimens replaced, so that they could be returned to the factory and accounted for? The replacement material was some mix prepared by your father, the extraordinary tinkerer, and brought into the factory in your trucks with the food you provided for the cafeteria. Simple. Perfect."

— "So come work for my Dad. Your three million will double."

— "No, I'd be afraid to end like Piesecki. But I haven't got to what I really want to tell you. Your father confessed to me that he was with Piesecki when Piesecki killed my son and his partner. He told you on the phone that he would confess, he told you to be strong, Didn't he, Little Babushka?" John paused to wait for a confirmation or a denial but there was only silence. "And your father left a written confession and took the blame so the security tapes in your building would not be viewed by the detectives. Why? Because it was not Piesecki who went up the elevator with your father to retrieve the target pistol, it was you Little Babushka. It was you who picked up your father in front of Jack's building, Piesecki had left by himself. It was you who drove your father home. It was you in the elevator. Your father went to his floor to get the target pistol and fetch a pair of bottles of Champagne while you raided your refrigerator for food to take along. The tape would have showed the pair of you carrying bags. It was you who got behind Christian and my Jack to shoot them in the head. Did your father actually take a photograph?" John checked the chronometer, four minutes left. "Go ahead deny it."

— "My father has the best lawyers in the country, my father will be fine."

" — This is the best part Julie Taylor, listen good. You have one thousand kilos of pure SA-286 laying on the floor of your saloon. The Immigration guys you met this afternoon were not Immigration guys, they were Christian's uncle's guys. One of them boarded your boat, opened one of the boxes, took half of the contents out and placed this wonderful device in the box and sealed it back, eight screws seal the top. Are you with me Julie Taylor? Soon you will hear a soft whistle, it's the oxygen being released, ten seconds later two fluids will mix and there will be a small explosion, small but large enough to ignite the SA-286 left in the box, and then the rest of the boxes, and fifteen thousand gallons of diesel, you'll be vaporized. One last thing, your father will not need any lawyers. Your father splashed himself on the pavement, he jumped from his penthouse. And don't worry about your mother, Julie, your mother is dead too, your father killed her. Listen for that whistle, Julie"."

Julie dropped the telephone and screamed at the top of her lungs as she run for the stern. She heard the whistle half way to the sliding doors leading to the rear deck. Julie never reached the doors.

John did not hear the sound of the explosion, the satellite telephone just went silent. There was no sound that reached Monty's boat either, nor a light in the distance. It was like it did not happen, but it did. The five men remained silent for a few minutes. Revenge is never as satisfying as one expects it to be.

Chapter 14
In the Line of Duty

— "Tony, get to the car and bring me my cigarettes." So Gorilla Number Two actually has a name. The two big men had sat at the side bench, one on each side of Monty, and this looked like an apricot squeezed between two very large pineapples. Tony had to turn sideways to make it through the narrow door. "Remember I told you I had a contract for one hundred grand for the one who killed my Christian, you've earned Johnny. Tony went to get you the envelope. Don't blow it all in Hawaii."

— "You going to Hawaii John?" Monty sounded happy.

— "That's the date I told you about, four weeks."

— "With the detective?"

John felt uncomfortable with the chit-chat, meaningless words just to avoid silence. "Yeah, Carol."

Monty moved away from Gorilla Number One and stretched both arms. "What was that you said about boxes?" Monty stretched his legs and bent forward to touch his toes with his hands.

— "Julie had loaded a thousand kilos of their wonderful explosive on her boat. They were on their way to unload at some harbor in Michigan or Wisconsin and then trucking it. Final destination Marseille, France."

— "To sell it in Europe. Maybe the Middle East? Terrorists?"

— "No, Taylor fashioned himself as a Serbian patriot, same with the guy Taylor sent to kill me."

— "Serbian patriots? Another killer?"

— "Taylor, his father, Taylor's wife and Julie too, they fed the explosives to a group of Serbs in France, you know these people and their neighbors have been killing each other for centuries. The Taylors weren't selling the explosive, they were using it. Well, not anymore."

Gorilla Number Two returned with a thick envelope in his left hand and the poster wrapped in the red blanket John had taken from Jack's house under his right arm. He brought no cigarettes.

— "The envelope is for you Johnny, one hundred big ones. You have my thanks too." Tony untied the white cord and leaned the poster wrapped in the blanket on the cabinet in front of the bench. Monty prepared to be squeezed again as Tony readied his frame to sit down. The apricot was again locked between the two pineapples.

— "You did not get your cigarettes, Gianni." Monty was showing his discomfort, maybe the pineapples were too much for the apricot.

— "I quit smoking three years ago. Used the patch." Gianni reached for his cane as he played with the white cord. "Unwrap the picture Johnny."

John left the red blanket fall on the deck and leaned the black and white poster on the cabinet. "We brought this one for you Monty." It was the poster from Jack's and Christian's bedroom. "The one in the kitchen I'm taking with me to Florida. The poster is for the phone call."

— "You did not have to, that was nothing, I'm happy I helped you guys."

— "Not this phone call Monty, the other phone call."

— "What do you mean?"

— "I mean the phone call you made to Jack's house from your office the day Jack and Christian were killed. You told me yourself that you called Jack's house while Taylor was in your office. Telling me was your big mistake Monty, it took Jack at least half an hour to get home, so Taylor stayed in your office for that long. You sold your friends out Monty, you're a Judas, you did it for forty coins of silver. You got Taylor's contract to pay for your betrayal and the contract was going to get you your new boat. You telephoned Jack and you told him you were coming over with Taylor to settle Taylor's problem, that Taylor had agreed to disclose the loss of explosives to the Army. Isn't that what you told Jack? And Jack believed you, Didn't he? Why not? You were not just his boss, you were his friend, your good and trusted friend. Isn't that what you said to Gianni before?"

— "I didn't know Taylor would kill them. How would I know that?" Thick drops of perspiration were coming down Monty's forehead."

The two big men grabbed Monty under his armpits and stood up as they lifted Monty, who hung trembling with his feet inches off the deck. "And when Taylor and his daughter showed up with two bottles of Champagne Jack let them in and the four of them sat down to sip wine and eat sushi as they waited for you to arrive. Do you want to know how Julie did it? Because it was beautiful Julie that killed Jack and Christian, not Taylor. Julie crouched behind the sofa so Taylor would take a photograph of her with our two boys." Gianni slid his heavy cane inside Monty' sweat shirt behind Monty's head and pushed the cane down to Monty's waist. "You betrayed your friends Monty, you have to pay for both of them." Gianni DiRenzo stood behind Monty and wrapped the white cord around Monty's neck. "You'll die looking at Jack's and Christian's picture."

DiRenzo had tied the white cord's ends and used a short piece of bamboo to turn the cord and make it tight around Monty's neck. "I cut this piece from the fishing pole Christian gave me for my birthday when he was twelve." DiRenzo turned the stick slowly and Monty turned his head right and left and kicked furiously front and back with both legs hitting DiRenzo with his heels, who repeated "Christian, Christian, …" until Monty's head was pressed against the cane and there were no more kicks. DiRenzo did not untie the cord, he gave it four more turns and pulled a piece of soft wire from his pocket to tie the stick to the cane. Monty' remains would never be found, it would be assumed that Monty had sailed in Taylor's yacht.

No words were said. John had to help DiRenzo negotiate his way to the dock without the cane. The two big men would carry Monty's body to one of the cars. "I'll be seeing you Johnny." John spent what remained of the night at Patrick's house and in the early afternoon drove to Carol's. Their flight would leave at six sharp, they were changing planes in San Diego. The newspapers carried a big spread about Taylor's murder-suicide but nothing yet about Taylor's yacht. Maybe tomorrow.

— "I'll call this our third date, and the fourth will be dinner at the airport in San Diego. What d' you say?"

— "I say goody, and I want you to know that I already forgave you for being at the yacht after the party."

— "Forgave me? For what?"

— "John, you were going to bed the skinny bitch. I know that, but I forgive you. Because you were going to bed her in the line of duty."